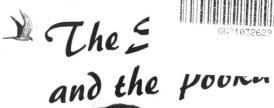

The and the pooka

Patrick Devaney

MENTOR PRESS

This Edition first published 1996 by

Mentor Press

43 Furze Road,
Sandyford Industrial Estate,
Dublin 18.

Tel. (01) 295 2112/3   Fax. (01) 295 2114

ISBN : 0 947548 85 8

1 3 5 7 9 10 8 6 4 2

Cover and Text Illustrations: Don Conroy

Printed in Ireland by ColourBooks

CONTENTS

for

Clare, Catherine, Deirdre,
Aileen and Conor

Acknowledgments

My thanks are due to my wife, Cheryl, for helpful comments and criticisms; to my children for demonstrations of modern English usage; to Teresa Leak for a statue of Ganesha; to Don Conroy for his illustrations; to my editors, Daniel McCarthy and John McCormack for professional advice and suggestions and to Catherine Heslin for efficiently typing the manuscript; to Harvard University Press for the quotation from *"The Wish of Manchín of Liath"*, from Kenneth Jackson's *A Celtic Miscellany*, and to Penguin Books for the quotation from Laurens Van Der Post's *The Heart of the Hunter*.

"I wish, O son of the Living God,
ancient eternal King, for a
secret hut in the wilderness
that it may be my dwelling."

from *"The Wish of Manchín of Liath"*
Translated from the Irish (9th Century) by Kenneth Jackson

"… we ourselves, whether we know it or not,
need to follow also the animal, the first thing
in ourselves, to arrive at a more authoritative
statement of life and personality."

Laurens Van Der Post
The Heart of the Hunter

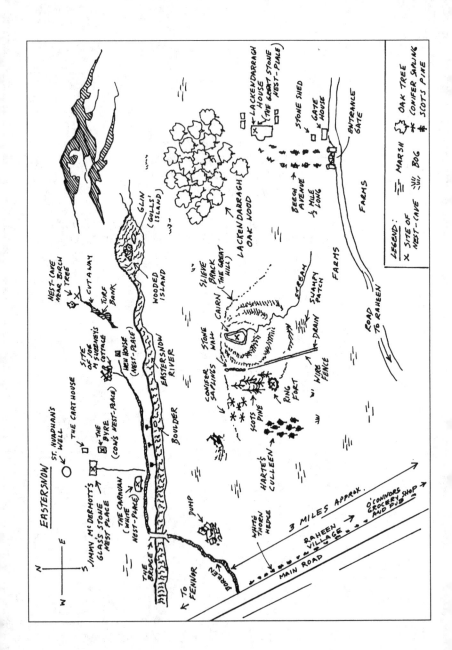

Prologue

Kok-kok-kok! Kok-kok! With a guttural crow a dark brown bird exploded from the heather, startling the boys into silence. Then as they recovered their wits, they roared their excitement: "Blazes! Wow! Bloody pigeon! No, it's a grouse! Look, it's gliding! If I had a shotgun - Pow! I bet there's a nest".

Quartering the ground like gundogs, the six boys ranged over and back, squelching through wet moss or striding through woody ling that brushed their knees. Suddenly another grouse exploded into flight. It was so close they could plainly see its barred yellow feathers.

"That's the hen!" Johnny O'Rourke, a gangling fellow with a shaven head, proclaimed. At fifteen, Johnno, as he was called, was the oldest of the boys and was looked up to for his hard-man attitude. That morning instead of attending mass, he had led them to Lough Glin, where there was a colony of Black-Headed Gulls. Big Jim Burke had told him that he had seen birds with red bills among the gulls and Johnno wanted to see these strange newcomers for himself. When the boat in which they had planned to row to the gulls' island sprang a leak, they had pushed it out past the reeds and watched while it filled with water. Then to console themselves for their bad luck, they had pelted a swan's nest and a moorhen's nest with stones. It had been great craic, especially when the male swan had come charging towards them, battering the water with his wings and hissing angrily. Now there was a chance for more fun.

"Keep looking, lads!" Johnno called out. "Did ye see how the hen lit over there instead of heading for Slieve Brack? She knows we're near the nest."

Bending down, the boys parted the thicker clumps of heather with their hands, peering into the interiors. Patiently they combed every square foot of cover but if there was a nest, it was too well hidden.

"We might as well call it a day," Johnno's mate, P.J., lit a fag.

"Yes," Gallo, a swarthy, well-built youth, agreed. "I'm knackered."

"Okay," Johnno turned back towards Eastersnow, where they had left their bikes. Before the group had time to follow, however, there was a cry from one of their number.

"Here, lads!" a slender boy with curly, brown hair squatted in front of a hummock. They rushed over and bent in a half circle to get a better view. There in a hollow under the lea of thick heather they could just make out a clutch of buff-coloured eggs, mottled with brown.

"Wow!" Freddy, the youngest boy, gave voice to their wonder.

"We must have flushed her before she had time to cover them," the slender boy's eyes were shining.

"Here, let me see!" Johnno pulled him back and grabbed one of the eggs.

"Don't do that!" the slender boy pleaded. "If she gets your smell, she'll desert the nest."

The group sniggered and in a flash of temper Johnno smashed the egg on the slender boy's head. "Now she'll get your smell, O'Connor," he crowed as the yellow yolk ran down the curly brown hair.

Taking their cue from their leader, the other boys grabbed an egg each but because they hoped to sell them to egg collectors, they held them carefully or slipped them into their pockets. There were only two eggs left in the nest and the slender boy tried to shield them.

"Get back, O'Connor, or I'll flatten you!" Johnno warned.

"Oh, leave him alone, O'Rourke," a stocky boy with shoulder-length hair remarked.

"No, I'll not leave him alone, Miller," Johnno didn't like his actions being questioned. "He was the same last year when we limed the goldfinches, letting them go and then claiming it was the Pooka. We don't have to listen to a lot of whinging from a mammy's -"

He got no further. With an unexpected lunge, O'Connor grabbed the heels of his wellingtons and hitting his knees with his shoulder, knocked him backwards. Like a wildcat, Johnno recoiled and sinking his fingers in O'Connor's hair, dragged him towards the nest. Before he could push his face into the remaining eggs, however, there was an eerie scream and he froze. The scream was repeated, a thin piercing cry like the distress call of a young animal or bird, then it changed to a long, wavering wail that seemed to come from different spots, now from a patch of sedge, now from a clump of dwarf willows, now from a heathery hummock.

"Didn't I tell you there was a Pooka?" O'Connor gasped, trying to pry Johnno's fingers from his hair.

"Over there, lads!" Johnno released his victim and went plunging off in the direction of the last call, followed by most of the boys.

"Here, Aidan," Miller handed an egg to O'Connor. "You can put mine back."

As Aidan placed the egg carefully in the nest the eerie cry rang out again, but further off, as if whatever creature was making it were retreating towards the lake.

"It's probably a hare being chased by a weasel," Miller didn't sound very certain. "Look, Aidan! Look!" He pointed to a flock of gulls and terns that, attracted by the cries, were heading towards the racing boys.

Intent on their search, Johnno and his companions failed to notice the new arrivals till it was too late. Screaming shrilly, the birds swooped down, wheeling and twisting within inches of the boys' faces. Johnno flailed at a gull with his fists but a tern zoomed in from the rear and, in passing, struck his head with his bill, leaving a red streak along the shaven crown. The other boys fared no better. As if maddened by the distress call of the hidden creature, the flock dive-bombed the cursing, stumbling vandals, driving them into headlong retreat. Aidan and Miller lay face down in the heather and though a few gulls veered over them, they were not attacked.

On and on the pursuit went, Johnno and his henchmen falling repeatedly into moss-pools and blind drains. It was not until they were almost out of sight on the western fringe of the bog that the eerie cry rang out once more and the flock wheeling upward, headed back to Lough Glin.

"Jeepers," Miller exclaimed as they got to their feet, "whatever made those cries must be able to savvy bird lingo."

"Didn't I tell you it was the Pooka?" Aidan looked around fearfully before tiptoeing away with his companion. After the recent uproar, the singing of larks and meadow pipits seemed like nature's attempt to pretend that nothing unusual had happened.

CHAPTER 1

When Maeve came to a point where the whitethorn hedge bordering the road petered out she set down her heavy case. For a moment the vast brown wilderness of bog rising gradually to snow-capped mountains filled her with dismay, then she recollected that this was what she had come to find. Somewhere out there was Eastersnow, the spot where she had elected to spend the rest of her life. If she lost her nerve now, it would mean that all her critics were right: the notion of a young woman living as a hermit in the last decade of the Twentieth Century was simply madness.

Maeve shifted the knapsack on her back to try to gain some relief from the straps biting into her shoulders. For a moment the image of barefooted Indians chewing coca leaves while carrying enormous loads up mountain paths flashed into her mind - if the Indians could do that, why couldn't she? But no, she had put all that business behind her - no slipping back at the first hint of pain.

While she was inspecting the sky for rain clouds, she noticed in the distance a falcon hovering above the heather. What was it waiting to swoop down on? A field mouse or a tiny bird? Maybe a poor little sparrow like the one she had rescued from Tom, her cat? If God worried about the fall of a sparrow, why had He created the falcon? It was a mystery like the other mysteries that had troubled her while working for GIVE: why did God allow some people to starve while others had to worry about dieting and why did people like Mr. Hunt live in beautiful Eighteenth Century mansions while

Travellers shivered in caravans by the side of the road?

Suddenly a blackbird broke into song and joy reawakened in her heart. Lifting up the case she resumed the journey. It was essential that she press on, otherwise she might have to spend the night in the open. A woman in the village of Raheen, where the bus had set her down, had offered to drive her out to Eastersnow. Why had she refused? Surely she must have walked four miles already?

After trudging for what seemed ages, she came at last to a rutted track leading off to the right. Was this the boreen the woman had mentioned? Yes, it must be, because there was a peak that fitted the description of Slieve Brack dominating the middle distance and a river that must be the Eastersnow snaking its boulder-strewn course through an endless expanse of sedge and heather.

A printed notice nailed to the trunk of a whitethorn by the roadside caught her eye:

£500 REWARD
FOR INFORMATION
ON TREE VANDALS
CONTACT J. BURKE, RAHEEN

Was J. Burke Mr. Hunt's foreman? The notice disturbed her, reminding her of all the ugly things she had left Dublin to escape. She scanned the bog for trees but apart from an occasional clump of what might be birches or willows, couldn't see any plantation.

At the northern side of the valley an abandoned farmhouse with a slated roof stood in forlorn isolation. Nearer the river, just as Eileen McGreevy, her boss at GIVE, had described it, a caravan rested like a white shoe box amid its primeval surroundings.

"Mr. Hunt says you are welcome to it till the end of May," Eileen had told her. "His foreman, Mr. Burke, will be needing it then - I understand Mr. Burke is afraid the village boys may vandalise it if it's left empty."

"And Mr. Hunt owns the land around it?" Maeve had put on her innocent look.

"Yes," Eileen nodded. "He owns all the land from Eastersnow back to Lackendarragh Wood."

Maeve was about to ask what the foreman would be doing while living in the caravan, then thought better of it. Mr. Hunt was a generous supporter of GIVE but if he ever learned that, in addition to working for that organisation, she was also a freelance journalist, he might have second thoughts about helping her. Fortunately, her articles had been published under the pen name Silvia, so only her friends in the Green movement knew of her other occupation. She recalled an article she had written condemning Mr. Hunt's company for importing hardwoods from Africa. Was she being a hypocrite then in accepting his generosity? No, she decided, since from now on she would be devoting all her energies to doing what she always wanted to do, painting.

As she walked down the boreen a raw breeze made her eyes water. She passed a spot where, among cotton grass and mosses, cars and vans had been dumped. How would Silvia have reported this? EYESORE THREATENS EDEN? At last she came to a crude bridge made of iron girders across which heavy planks had been laid. The wood echoed hollowly under her shoes as she passed over the slow-moving river. Then she was on the far side and walking across brown peat sparsely covered with heather to which the withered blossoms still clung.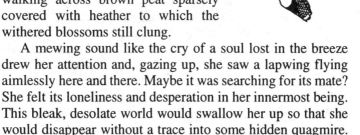

A mewing sound like the cry of a soul lost in the breeze drew her attention and, gazing up, she saw a lapwing flying aimlessly here and there. Maybe it was searching for its mate? She felt its loneliness and desperation in her innermost being. This bleak, desolate world would swallow her up so that she would disappear without a trace into some hidden quagmire. To add to her unease, rain began to fall, a light drizzle that clung to her hair and denim dress. "I'm not turning back," she kept repeating like an incantation. CREECH! CREECH! A snipe rose suddenly from a moss-pool, almost scaring her to death. It zigzagged away into the grey sky, leaving her feeling even more abandoned. What was she, a girl born and reared in the city, doing in this sodden waste with no other human being within miles?

Clumps of whins with yellow blossoms growing near the side of the track added the first touch of colour she had seen since leaving Raheen. There was something hostile and fierce about their thorny branches. By the river's edge bullrushes stood forlornly, their brown mace-heads bursting into cotton fluff. An occasional sally tree rose from the flat expanse of heather but the soil was too barren to allow them to reach any great height.

When she was near the caravan she came on three clumps of daffodils. What a surprise to find daffodils in bloom so late in April and, furthermore, to find them out here in the bog? An image of her mother bent over flowers in the back garden rose in her mind, then she pushed it away.

With renewed determination she quickened her pace and was soon turning the key in the caravan door. The inside smelled musty but it was neat. In no time she had lit the gas heater and was enjoying the sandwiches and orange drink she had brought with her. She had always been a light eater - except on those occasions when things had become too much. Well, from now on it would be hermit fare!

She spent the few remaining hours of daylight airing the sheets and blankets of the divan bed and laying out her possessions. Among the latter was a small ivory statue of Ganesha, the elephant-headed god to whom Hindus pray when starting a new enterprise. Finally, she removed the blue denim dress, then bundled up in her underclothes and pyjamas, wriggled into bed and closed her eyes.

CHAPTER 2

When he heard Naoscach the Snipe call out in alarm Gerg rose to a crouched position, the half-eaten root of a silverweed clutched in his hand. Brushing the dark, matted locks from his forehead with grimy fingers, he stared down towards the distant river. At first the mist obscured his vision, then his hazel-flecked eyes detected movement beyond the tiny white nest-place left by the crutins in the last heather-bloom season but one. He drew in the breeze through distended nostrils but no taint of crutin rose from the valley. There was not even the smell of fire - you could usually tell by the stench of burning or the faint upcoil of smoke if the white nest-place was occupied. Nevertheless, something was moving.

Dropping to all fours he loped along the face of the hill, weaving among clumps of heather and around rocks as easily as a fox. The tattered sack covering his body blended well with his surroundings. Only a frog hiding in a clump of moss and Bran the Raven, riding the air currents above the western slope of Slieve Brack took note of his passing.

In a few minutes Gerg was half a mile closer to the white nest-place. Hunkering by a whin bush he was just in time to observe a slender crutin pause on the step before the nest entrance. A whimper escaped his lips. Nooma! Surely it was none other? The crutin had just her height and shape, though the blue covering she wore was strange. He watched while the newcomer stepped inside and closed the opening behind her. Then curbing his excitement, he made his way furtively to the river.

At a spot where a large boulder divided the current he paused, gauged the distance with his eye, then retreating from the bank, he raced forward and sprang. With sure-footed grace he landed on the wet surface of the boulder, then sprang again so that his momentum carried him within reach of an alder on the opposite bank. Grabbing a branch, he swung his flying body upward, at the last moment releasing his hold so that he flopped down safely in a clump of long grass. It was a feat of agility that few crutins could have matched, yet Gerg scarcely gave it a thought. When the weather was warm he usually waded or swam across the river, preferring to avoid the bridge. Like all gagna, or wild creatures, he distrusted anything that smelled of crutin and if it were not for the memory of Nooma drawing him on, he would not have ventured into their territory during suntime.

Now that he was within a stone's throw of the white nest-place, he sniffed the air but the rain had washed away any scents that would have told him more about the new arrival. Should he creep closer? No, there was always the chance that the female crutin might be waiting with a thunder-stick. He had seen many of his friends die painful, lingering deaths or crumple instantly into bloody heaps after the thunder-sticks discharged their lightning. There was also the danger of traps. On one dreadful sunup he had blundered into a trap set outside the nest-cave he was sharing with Duach the Badger and its steel jaws had bitten off his little finger so that there was now only a purple stump. After that he always took care to check for the smell of steel and when he found it merged with the odour of freshly disturbed clay he would throw a pebble at the spot, causing the trap to snap harmlessly. Since Glas, the grey crutin, had left his stone nest-place, however, there had been no trap smells.

Rain trickled down his face and neck, worked its way down his thin body beneath the sodden sack and joined the drops falling on his bare thighs and legs. He shook himself like a dog after emerging from water, wishing he were back in the dry comfort of his nest-cave on Slieve Brack. Then he recalled Glas's byre. He would shelter there till darkness fell.

Dropping onto all fours so that he would be difficult to detect, he crept through the heather, pausing occasionally to

18

check for enemies. Nothing stirred in that brown, desolate landscape, not even a greycrow. The scent of Giorria the Hare rose faintly from a hummock and from further off came the pungent odour of Sionnach the Fox but there was no smell of blood. As he neared Glas's stone nest-place, Naoscach rose with a startled screech from an overgrown drain, causing him to freeze, ears straining. When no sound of danger reached him, he resumed his advance.

Circling the stone nest-place to make sure it was unoccupied, he approached the byre, walking upright. Anyone watching from the white nest-place would have difficulty distinguishing him from the grey walls. Gently he eased back the bolt and peered into the dim interior. Smells of dry cow-dung and musty fodder mingled with the stench of owl pellets.

"Go bak bak bak!" instinctively he called out his grouse challenge. From the back of the loft Demna the Barn Owl hissed a startled protest.

To calm Demna, Gerg made the snoring sound young owls make when begging for food. The ploy worked. Demna flew out on ghostly wings to a rafter above the area where Bo the Cow used to be tied. When she peered down at Gerg he repeated the snoring sound and she gave a low yap of recognition.

For as many seasons of dead plants as there were fingers on his good hand Gerg had sheltered in the byre. During the last of these seasons Demna had arrived, floating in one sunup through the rectangular manure hole just as Gerg was about to slip out. After a few more encounters, Demna got used to his presence but because she was usually out hunting while he slept, he did not befriend her.

Removing his sack, Gerg threw it over a cross-beam, causing Demna to flutter to a new roost on the wall, directly under the galvanised iron roof. The air blowing through the manure hole made his moist skin gather into goose pimples. He swung himself up onto the crossbeam and jumped to the loft, which was over the area where the hay and turnips were stored. Locating the pile of sacks made from thick hessian that Glas kept for carrying turnips and potatoes, he draped one over his shoulders before sitting down on the others. A spider crawled up his thigh and he picked it up and ate it. Where was Glas now?

One sundown when Gerg had crept in through the manure hole Bo was not in the byre and not long afterwards Madra the dog went missing. Then about the time new buds were showing on the willows Glas himself disappeared. His stone nest-place no longer sent up smoke and no hens foraged near it. And now Nooma had come back. Could she have locked up Glas and Madra and the others in a secret nest-place where nobody would ever find them? The thought seared his mind.

"Gobak! Gobak! Gobak bak bak!" he called out in a sudden explosion of anger that made Demna hiss in alarm.

Clasping his hands about his knees he began to rock himself back and forth, whimpering plaintively. Demna watched him. She had a newly-laid egg in a nest at the back of the loft and she feared he might break it.

Gerg continued to rock and whimper while darkness thickened, then an unearthly screech roused him. It was Demna. She had floated unnoticed through the manure hole and was now hunting outside. He wished that he too had feathers so that he could wander freely across the bog, gliding over streams and moss-pools till he reached the island in the Bright Lake. The thought of feathers made him aware of the cold.

Taking the sack from his shoulders, he ripped neck and arm holes in it with his teeth and fingers and put it on. Quietly he dropped to the ground and tiptoed out of the byre. Everything seemed peaceful. The only sounds were the sighing of the breeze through the heather and the far-off cry of a passing curlew.

"Nooma, Nooma," he intoned silently, heading towards the dim outline of the white nest-place.

At first the patter of rain and sighing of the breeze had kept Maeve awake but gradually exhaustion carried her into a vast, empty darkness, through which her mind wandered restlessly. Towards midnight she woke up. What was that? Something prowling about the caravan? A man? Then her blood froze. An eerie singing, unlike anything she had ever heard, was issuing from the darkness outside, a mixture of bird notes and mewings and squeaks, as if some creature incapable of human sounds was crying out to her in despair. The voice fell silent, to be replaced by faint scratching sounds at the window, then it rose again, a little lost bleating, almost like *mam ma mam ma*, which tore at her heart. Presently the singing began again, rising and falling, changing to a kind of crowing: Gobak bak bak! Gobak! Gobak!

Blessing herself, she slipped out of bed and tiptoed to the window. There was a scurrying noise such as a frightened sheep or dog might make but when she looked out all she could see was the shadowy outline of sally bushes and heather clumps in the dim starlight.

CHAPTER 3

Light streaming through the lace curtains woke Maeve. The first thing she heard was a bird, that had to be a skylark, singing. In Dublin she often overslept and then her eardrums would be assaulted by a radio blaring in the upstairs flat or the whining of a hoover. Despite her frightful experience she had slept well. "Thank you, Ganesha," she addressed the statue with its four arms and crowned elephant's head standing on her bedside locker. He didn't move, too deep in contemplation to hear her!

As soon as she pushed back the blankets she became aware of the cold, a cold that seemed, however, to increase her sense of being alive. Dressing quickly, she opened the door. The sky was chilly blue with scattered white clouds. Now that the rain had passed, the countryside looked more than ever like a vast brown desert stretching away to the snow-capped mountains. Eileen had told her that "Eastersnow" was derived from *Diosart Nuadhan*, the desert of Nuadhan - was the place just like this when the hermit came here in the Sixth Century? It was certainly a beautiful vista, with no sign of man's presence.

On impulse she decided to check around the caravan for footprints, though in clear daylight she began to doubt the reality of what had happened during the hours of darkness. Maybe it was just a stray cat and her mind had played tricks on her? She recalled the almost human cries of Tom the Cat during his nocturnal trysts and smiled at her own foolishness. Pulling on her wellingtons, she carefully descended the two wooden steps to the ground. Then she saw something that told her she hadn't been hallucinating, prints in a patch of black mud.

Fingering the ankh hanging by a chain from her neck to

dispel her panic, she bent down. The depressions in the mud had partly closed in so that the outlines were no longer clear. What could have made such prints? A barefooted child or a chimp? She had heard Cheetah in a Tarzan movie gibbering and screaming. Maybe it was some animal like that.

"Steady, Maeve," she warned herself. "It was probably only some young brat trying to put the wind up you."

A musical clamour drew her attention and looking up, she saw a flock of swans flying north across the river. There was something so wild and pristine about the sight that, forgetting the disturbing prints, she raised her arms in rapture. It was as if God were showing her what the world was like before the fall of Adam. She watched till the swans melted into the haze above where she reckoned Fennor, the county town, lay. Then hurrying inside, she took out her watercolours and artist's pad and made a quick likeness of the scene she had just witnessed.

Leaving the picture to dry, she thought of breakfast, only to recall that, except for a few biscuits, she had no food. She would have to walk to Raheen and purchase enough bread and canned beans to last till the weekend. By then she would have some idea how to supplement her diet with wild plants: chickweed, nettles and watercress. In Dublin she had often lived for days on water and muesli. Indeed, it was her refusal to eat after she had seen starving African children on T.V. that had convinced Eileen that she was taking her work for GIVE too much to heart. Maybe a spell living in Eastersnow would bring her to her senses or, as Eileen put it, "If it doesn't kill you, me girl, that bog air will certainly restore your appetite." Maeve smiled. Whatever about food, she needed drinking water. She would try to find the well which the people of the farmhouse must have used.

In a few minutes she was walking along the rutted track north of the caravan, a plastic bucket in her hand. She scanned the farmhouse chimney for any wisp of smoke but there was none and she could discern grass growing on its top. The windows also had that blank appearance which proclaims the absence of life. On peering through a dirty pane her judgement was confirmed; the crude furniture was covered with a film of dust and the hearth was bare, the black crane without pot or kettle.

As she was turning away from the house, she noticed that the byre door was ajar. Suppressing an impulse to flee, she approached and pushed it further in. Immediately a dirty, wet potato sack hanging from a beam caught her eye. "Anybody home?" she called out. There was no answer. Undeterred by the rank smells, she walked in and gingerly removed the sack, noting as she did so the large, untidy holes that resembled arm and neck openings. Her mind more troubled than ever, she retreated from the byre, occasionally looking back over her shoulder.

She was lifting a bucket of water from the river when children's voices made her raise her head. A boy and girl were cycling across the bridge. They dismounted when they got closer and she could see a bulging cardboard box tied to the carrier of each bike.

"Good morning, Miss," they answered her greeting shyly.

"What brings you out here?" she enquired after they had introduced themselves. The boy, whose name was Aidan, told her that their parents, Mr. and Mrs. O'Connor who owned the grocery shop in Raheen, had sent them out before school with food.

"But I didn't order any," she was puzzled.

"That's all right," the girl, whose name was Eithne, assured her. "Mr. Hunt phoned daddy last night and said he would pay for everything."

Now she understood: Eileen was worried that she would starve and had contacted Mr. Hunt. Her first impulse was to tell them that she had no intention of accepting Mr. Hunt's charity but they seemed such pleasant children it would be unfair to upset them.

They carried the boxes into the caravan, chatting more freely as they warmed to her. Eithne, a pretty dark-haired girl with frank blue eyes, was in her last year in National School and was going to attend the convent in Fennor in the coming autumn. Aidan, whose curly brown hair and mischievous grey-brown eyes reminded her of her own brother, Danny, was in Fifth class in the National School and eleven years old, a year younger than his sister.

"What will you do here?" Eithne was gazing at the picture of the swans.

"Paint," Maeve confessed. "That's my first effort. What do you think of it?"

"It's cool," Eithne seemed genuinely impressed. "I wish I could paint like that."

When she asked about the well, they brought her to a depression in the field behind the farmhouse, where there was a flat, cleft rock with a tiny cross incised on it. The water in the cleft was brownish but tasted good. The children did not know if the well had any connection with Saint Nuadhan, though they remembered that Jimmy Mac Dermott, who used to live in the farmhouse, had told them that the cross had been there in his grandfather's time.

It was now approaching eight-thirty and the children were anxious to be off, as school started at nine-fifteen. Before they left, she showed them the potato sack and footprints and casually mentioned the sounds she had heard during the night. To her amazement, they became visually uneasy.

"You shouldn't be staying out here on your own, Miss," Eithne sounded very grown-up for her years, "Anybody could be roaming the bog at night."

"But it was obviously a prankster," Maeve spoke dismissively. "Have you heard of such things before?"

"Yes, Miss," Aidan ignored his sister's frown. "It's the Pooka."

"The Pooka?" Maeve didn't understand.

"Oh, Aidan, that's nonsense!" Eithne said disdainfully.

"No, it's not," Aidan insisted. "I told you about the seagulls, didn't I? And you yourself saw the cut on Johnno's head."

"Just because seagulls attacked you, that doesn't prove anything," Eithne pointed out. "Did you see the Pooka?"

"No, I didn't," Aidan conceded. "But Jimmy Mac Dermott did."

"Oh, for Pete's sake! You don't believe the likes of Jimmy?" Eithne was exasperated.

"What about the young trees that were pulled up and the torn plastic turf bags?" Aidan demanded hotly. "Is that nonsense too?"

CHAPTER 4

When he heard the female crutin tiptoe to the window Gerg fled in blind panic. Bounding along the track that was visible in the starlight, he was soon far beyond the white nest-place. At the alder where he had crossed the river the previous suntime he slowed down, panting. If it was Nooma who had come back, she would be mad at him for having bothered her.

In the time before his escape Nooma had often been mad at him, locking him in after she gave him food, though he wanted to follow her. He would pound on the wooden door with his fists and cry to be let out but she would not relent. Eventually, tired and defeated, he would retreat into a corner, fold his arms about his knees and rock himself back and forth, whimpering.

Gradually the clucking of the hens whose nest-place he shared would soothe him and he would pet Suairc, the gentle one, and cluck back to her. In those times he could make few other sounds as Nooma never called to him. He would hear her footsteps and put his eye to the knothole in the door to watch for her. Presently she would appear, head down, his shiny bowl in her hand.

He would wait while she drew back the bolt and he would squat before her, clucking. When this happened she would gaze at him with such a strange look in her luminous eyes that he didn't know if she would pet or strike him. She would wait by the door while he lifted the bowl to his mouth and gulped down the gruel and milk. Occasionally there would be small lumps of meat in the bowl or bread crusts and potatoes such as the hens ate. Once when she found him sucking the yolk from an egg she snatched it out of his hand and stamped away without feeding him. After that he left the eggs alone.

When the weather grew cold she gave him an extra potato sack to wear, throwing it over a rafter as if she feared to touch him. When she cleaned out the nest-place - which she did every other suntime - she backed him into a corner while she scraped up the dirty bedding with a dung fork. Afterwards, she would spread fresh straw or hay on the floor, threatening him with the dung fork if he dared to move. Despite her efforts, he was always bothered by feather-lice that hid in the coarse cloth of the sacks.

Often when Gerg looked out through the knothole he saw Nooma with a giant crutin who walked with the aid of a stick. The giant would be making the mumbling sounds crutins make and Nooma would be listening or moving her hands. She never brought the giant to the nest-place, probably because she feared he would harm Gerg. Once Gerg had seen him hitting Lao the Calf with his stick and on another occasion throwing it at Minseach the Goat. It was because of the giant that he dreaded the outside world.

As he grew older, however, the desire for freedom overcame his dread. One suntime when the hens were foraging and he was all alone in the stifling hot gloom, he felt he could endure being locked up no longer. Rushing forward, he threw his full weight against the door. It gave a little. Encouraged, he continued to hit it with his bare shoulder till, with a rasping groan, it flew open and he went sprawling out onto the dirt.

For a moment he lay there, blinded by the light, then, picking himself up, he scrambled away on all fours just as the door of the crutins' nest-place opened and the giant emerged. He heard him calling Nooma but he did not stop. The sack he wore protected his body from heather twigs but his arms and face were soon stinging and his muscles ached from the unaccustomed exercise. When he reached some clamps of turf he collapsed behind one, gasping for breath.

After a while he peeped out. Nooma was standing by the hens' nest-place with a stick in her hand. He heard hollow, strangled grunting, as if she were trying to call out to him, but he did not trust her. She would lock him up again and this time so securely he would never escape. When she set off in his direction, he crept away through the heather and did not stop till he came to an area of withered moorgrass, where he hid till dusk. Then, tired and hungry, he curled up in a hummock of moss and fell asleep.

During star-time he jerked awake. A beam of light was bobbing and scything across the bog. It fell once or twice on his hummock but then passed on. He knew it was Nooma searching for him and an almost overpowering urge rose in his breast to cry out but he suppressed it. For the remaining hours of darkness a chill breeze kept him awake. He blundered around, trying to find a warmer roost. At sunup he went searching for food and came upon a teal's nest. Greedily he ate the eggs then, feeling drowsy, lay in the heather and slept.

He was awakened by chattering sounds. A number of crutins were doing something at the edge of the bog. Hunger goading him on, he crawled up close to them and saw that they were turning over black lumps of peat with their hands. Circling the area, his nose picked up the faint odour of food. Patiently he worked his way forward and by the unearthed stump of a tree discovered a bundle. He sniffed warily before touching it with his hand.

Keeping one eye on the crutins, he crawled away with his prize, freezing whenever their heads turned in his direction. At last he was safely beyond their view and with teeth and nails he ripped open the bundle and devoured the bread and meat inside.

For two more suntimes he remained in that area, eating the eggs of curlews and lapwings then hunger drove him back to Nooma's nest-place. As he drew near it, a great billowing cloud of smoke told him something was wrong. Venturing closer, he could see lurid tongues of flame flickering through the smoke. From behind a turf clamp he watched strange crutins throwing buckets of water on the flames but there was no sign of Nooma or the giant. Acrid fumes carried by a shift in the breeze stung his eyes and nostrils. Finally, with a great burst of sparks, the roof collapsed. After waiting for ages to see if Nooma would appear, he slunk away from the smouldering pile.

A short detour took him within sight of Glas's stone nest-place, where the aroma of freshly baked bread made his mouth dribble. Creeping up to the window he peeped in. There was no crutin to be seen. He went to the door and fumbled with the latch. To his surprise the door opened inward. Hesitantly, he tiptoed into the enormous, gloomy den with its pungent smells, unfamiliar furniture and smoking fire. A round, flat bread-lump rested on the table. Quick as a fox he pounced on it and bolted out the door.

For many moon seasons he remained near the stone nest-place, usually approaching it when darkness fell. After a while Madra the Dog welcomed him and there was always food to be had: eggs in the hens' nest-place, turnips and carrots in the cabbage garden, and, best of all, saucers of milk left on the windowsill at the onset of darkness. He would stand on tiptoe to look through the window at Glas sitting by the fire with a burning root-knob in his mouth, while Madra dozed near his feet. Now and then Glas removed the root-knob in order to spit into the ashes.

One time Madra woke up and sensing Gerg's presence, whined a greeting, whereupon Glas turned his head; when he spied Gerg's face at the window he let the burning root-knob drop from his mouth. A few moments later he came rushing out, carrying his thunder-stick. Gerg took to his heels. The thunder-stick exploded. Hidden by the darkness, he felt something whizzing past his head and nicking his ear. When he touched his ear it felt sticky. On and on he raced, Madra barking dutifully behind him. From then on Gerg was determined to avoid the vicinity of crutins, but in the seasons of dead plants the cold had always driven him back to Glas's byre.

It was near this very spot, Gerg recalled, that Madra had broken off the chase, wouffing to show there was no ill feeling. Other images from the past attacked him like angry bees: Nooma standing by the hens' nest-place with a stick, making horrible grunting sounds ... Glas trying to kill him with his thunder-stick ... Nooma entering the white nest-place - handing him the shiny bowl with blue trees and blue birds and tiny blue crutins on it ... Suairc clucking to him ... Nooma tiptoeing to the window while he sang to her - searching for him with the beam of light ... the giant's and Nooma's nest-place enveloped in flames ...

What had become of the shiny bowl? Maybe he should visit his old nest-place?

CHAPTER 5

As Gerg continued along the track that ran adjacent to the river his nostrils picked up the faint odour of Sionnach the Fox mingled with the odour of blood. The odour grew stronger. At last his nose led him to a dark form lying in the grass. It was Sionnach. From the rank smell he knew he had been dead more than one suntime. Crumale must have killed him with his thunder-stick. Gerg bared his teeth. Of all crutins he feared Crumale most, Crumale the cruel hunter of gagna, the destroyer of heather hens. If it were not for the loneliness gnawing at his insides he would have turned back.

The track swung to the left and brought him to a place of oblong shadows where Nooma and the giant had lived. He approached the smallest shadow. Though he could scarcely discern its outline, he knew that this was the hens' nest-place. Instantly, Suairc's image came back to him so that he clucked instinctively but there was no answering cluck. To distract his mind from the emptiness engulfing it, he listened to the night's voices: the soft whistle of Dobarchu the Otter from the river, a thin squeak uttered by Skeehawn the Bat in the murky sky overhead and further off, in the direction of Glas's farm, the lonely mewing of Plibeen the Lapwing.

Satisfied that there was no danger lurking around, he dropped onto all fours and crept up to the entrance, sniffing, peering. A barely perceptible odour of crutin mingled with the odour of damp earth. It was a warning: if he ventured inside Nooma would surely come and lock him in. Rising abruptly, he backed away. He would have to use his old nest-cave near the birch tree.

He had found this nest-cave when Crumale was pressing him hard. It was during the last but one season of ripe fruit, after Crumale had slaughtered the heather hens. In revenge Gerg had pulled up the young trees Crumale and his crutins had planted on the side of the Great Hill. Then to throw Crumale's dogs off his trail, he had swum across the river. If Crumale had found him, he would now be like Sionnach, a lifeless heap thrown in the grass.

Leaving the hens' nest-place, he padded on through moss and heather till he reached a line of turf banks. Carefully he eased his body down to the lower level and squelching past bogholes which bordered the cutaway, felt his way to a corner, where grass covered the mouth of the nest-cave. Unknown to Gerg, the "cave" had been dug by Glas to hide a poteen still. Over the years, the roof had partly collapsed but the inner chamber had been kept intact by a birch growing directly overhead. One sniff told Gerg that the cave was not occupied. Wriggling in headfirst, he was soon standing in the chamber. The damp floor was lined with plastic turf bags he himself had collected and the ceiling was festooned with roots. In one corner there was a pile of heather on which he used to sleep.

Groping his way to the pile he felt for the hazelnuts he had left there. He cracked a few with his teeth but the kernels were so bitter he spat them out. Without bothering to remove his filthy sack, he curled up on the heather and tried to sleep. After endless tossing and turning he found himself back in the hens' nest-place, clucking to Suairc. Nooma came with a bowl of gruel but when he had eaten it, she would not let him out, even though he whimpered and pounded on the door.

Then the door swung open. Instead of Nooma, however, the giant was there. His face looked like Crumale's and his cruel eyes were gleaming as he raised his stick. Gerg woke up, gasping with terror.

As awareness of where he was came flooding back, desolation filled his mind. Suairc was gone and Nooma did not want him. He longed for Suairceen, the heather hen he had reared from the time she was a chick to the time she was a poult. He had found her trapped in a crevasse made by the growling monsters with which crutins tear peat out of the bog. She was cheeping plaintively and almost dead from hunger. He had taken her back to his nest-place on the Great Hill and fed her with insects and caterpillars. Gradually she had grown stronger and he would bring her billberries and pieces of ling to eat and water in a plastic cup he had found near Glas's byre.

Soon she was foraging for herself in the heather on the Great Hill but every sundown she would return, creeping like a brown shadow up to his nest-place in the cairn. Looking at her he could feel himself sinking into a kind of trance in which his mind floated free of his body to mingle with hers. In such a state their cluckings would only give voice to what was already passing between them as the gurgling of water gives voice to the flowing of a stream. She would peck at the bunch of ling he held out to her before settling down contentedly to rest. And then one suntime he had heard thunder-sticks and after that he had seen her smooth form and bright, alert eye no more. Grief welled in him. Was he doomed to be always alone?

Sunlight was brightening the entrance to the nest-cave so he wriggled out and made his way to the river, where he drank from his cupped hands. After that he chewed sorrel and dandelion leaves and ate a few silverweed roots but hunger still gnawed at his stomach. Ignoring the chill, he lowered himself into the water and began churning the mud on the bottom with his feet. When the current was opaque he swam downstream, pausing to feel under shelves of rock and overhanging parts of the bank. Finally, he halted by a large boulder. Reaching under it with his arm he gently located a resting trout. With great skill he caressed the unseen fish, then with a quick flick he tossed it up onto the bank, where it jumped spasmodically. In a moment he had grabbed it in both hands and bitten it behind the head as Dobarchu the Otter does, killing it instantly. Squatting, he munched the succulent flesh till his hunger was satisfied.

Krark! Krark! a harsh squawking reached his ears. Gazing upwards he saw Corr the Heron being chased by Balor the Greycrow and his mate Babh. Were they trying to make Corr throw up whatever fish were in his craw? On and on the chase went, Corr twisting and turning to shake off the hooded bullies. Finally, the greycrows veered away and flew back to the whitethorn in which they had their nest. Gerg felt happy for his old friend, who was now winging slowly above the hazels of the culleen on the far side of the bog.

The attack on Corr reminded Gerg of the noisy crutins' raid on the heather fowl. Had the greycrows discovered broken eggs? If so, they might also have found the nest of Gorcock and Girsha. Looking around to make sure that no crutin was watching, he set off at an easy lope towards Lough Glin. When he came to within a hundred paces of the nest he gave a low chuckle. There was another chuckling call in answer. Dropping on all fours he padded forward through the heather and, sure enough, there was Gorcock standing guard on a hummock, red wattle gleaming above his dark shiny eye. That meant that Girsha was brooding the eggs. Unwilling to disturb her, he turned away. Then something occurred to him: suppose the same crutins that had attacked the nest of his friends should also attack Nooma's?

Gerg felt a cold chill. Why hadn't he thought of this before? She was all alone in the white nest-place. He would have to keep watch like Gorcock in case the noisy crutins returned. Forgetting his earlier panic, he headed back to Eastersnow.

CHAPTER 6

Maeve was thoughtful as she washed up after her meal of tinned salmon, bread and orange juice. It was very generous of Mr. Hunt to pay for the food, yet it had never been her intention to live on charity. She would have to get a nanny goat for milk and, maybe, plant vegetables if she couldn't find any edible plants growing wild. Then she had her painting - Kenny's gallery in Dublin had promised to take any water colours she sent. Mr. Kenny was also interested in illustrations for cards and books. The hundred pounds he had given her for a small landscape she had done last autumn was proof that she had talent. Once she had got over the first week here, she felt certain she would survive. If God looked after the birds of the air and the lilies of the field, he would not fail her.

Burying her face in water from the well, she patted it dry with a towel. Then, kneeling, she rummaged in her knapsack for a comb. In one corner her fingers touched a small packet wrapped in paper. For a moment she hesitated, remembering the highs in dimly-lit rooms throbbing with music. Unfortunately, the pleasure was always paid for next day in nausea and depression - and then there was the other cost: a week's pay blown on this tiny bit of junk ...

Rising, she put on her denim jacket and wellingtons and hurried to the river, where she watched the contents of the packet sink like poison through the amber current. The brown paper floated away like one of those Egyptian boats that carried the souls of the dead to the Other-world. Well, her soul wasn't embarking yet. Now that that phase of her life was behind her, it was time to explore her new world.

The boreen continued east of the turn-off for the farmhouse. She gazed around her as she walked, noting the signs of reawakening life: the yellow catkins on the sallies, fresh green leaves on a whitethorn, a daisy displaying its white petals, while, further off, snow still clung to the mountain tops. A wren broke into song in a patch of umber bracken and in the distance curlews filled the air with their clear, bubbling flute notes.

Where the boreen curved away from the river a dead fox was lying in the grass. There was blood on his muzzle and his tail was missing. She wrinkled her nose at the odour before moving on. Presently she came to a mound overgrown with nettles and briars. Somebody had erected a little wooden cross before it on which was written in white paint:

PRAY FOR THE SOULS OF
JOSEPH SWEENEY AND HIS
GRANDDAUGHTER NOREEN
R.I.P.

The paint was faded and the wood cracked by the sun, so the cross must have been set in place some years previously. It was strange coming on death out here, first the fox and then - Her eye fell on soot-blackened mortar and a charred rafter protruding from weeds. Immediately she understood the reason for the cross, the tragedy that had taken two lives at this isolated spot. How had the fire started? A spark falling on dry thatch? An oil lamp overturning?

Fingering her ankh, she circled the mound, discovering further evidence of fire where rabbits had burrowed: heat-cracked stones, pockets of grey ash. Sadness descended on her. Once there had been people living here; now there was nothing except the rabbits and, possibly, rats and mice. On impulse she picked two daisies and laid them before the cross. How uncertain life was ...

Beyond the mound she came on the ruins of outhouses, their thatched roofs fallen in and grass growing on the walls. A closer inspection revealed that one had been a carthouse, another a byre and another a stable. Further on there was a shed with a rusty galvanised iron roof, which had not collapsed. From the low walls and small trap door beside the main door opening, she guessed that this had been a henhouse. On peeping inside she could see the rotten remains of perches and nest boxes and what looked like a china bowl half buried in the dirt of the floor.

Gingerly she removed the bowl. It had a blue willow pattern. She would wash it thoroughly and keep it as a reminder of the people who had lived here. Perhaps she might plant flowers in it, violets or celandines or whatever bloomed in the acid peat of the bog.

As she was leaving the henhouse, she noticed bootprints near the door opening and what looked like the print of a small hand. Intrigued, she examined the ground outside. Near the west wall, the grass was trampled and there were cigarette butts and a spent cartridge case. So that was it! She recalled what she had learned while doing research for an anti-blood sports article. Whoever had killed the fox had waited here, probably with a powerful lamp and a recording of a squealing rabbit. When the fox approached, the lamp had been turned on and the dazzled animal shot. Sometime during the night the man and the child with him - the handprint was too small to be a man's - must have gone into the henhouse, possibly to shelter from a shower. Could the child be the same one that had visited her? No, that was unlikely.

Taking the bowl to a mosspool, she rinsed out the dirt. If it could speak would it tell a story as intriguing as the story depicted on its surface? Hadn't the Chinese heroine of that story, Koong-se, set her house on fire after her lover had been murdered, so that she died in the flames? And hadn't Noreen Sweeney and her grandfather died in a burning house? But she didn't know for certain if that was how they had died - and, yet, life was often stranger than fiction. Who would have imagined that she, at one time the bane of her parents' lives with her tantrums, her desire for fashionable clothes and her refusal to study, would be now a hermit-artist living in this wilderness? Would she have believed it herself when she was a teenager and saw herself as somebody like Koong-se, kept imprisoned by an angry father? And where would she be in ten years' time? Would she be a famous artist living in Jimmy Mac Dermott's farmhouse? She could use the money from her paintings to renovate it - with bigger windows the bedroom could be turned into a studio and she could ask Danny to come and live with her ... But she was letting her imagination get out of control: Danny wasn't coming back from Australia ...

The sun was now half-way down the cloudy grey sky; she would only walk a little further before turning back. At a spot where turf clamps had crumbled into heaps of black mould she was startled by a loud crowing: Go bak bak bak! Go bak! Go bak! The sound was so like that which had finished the medley of the previous night that she froze in her tracks. When the crow wasn't repeated, she began to tiptoe forward. Suddenly a dark bird exploded from the heather about thirty yards away and calling out "kok-kok-kok" in a guttural voice, went rocketing over the bog, now beating its wings rapidly, now holding them in a downward arc as it glided along.

With a thrill of delight she watched till the retreating bird had merged into the brown desert. What could it be? A pheasant? No, a pheasant had a long tail and a bigger body. It must be a grouse or a partridge. But would such a creature be able to mimic other creatures the way a parrot could mimic the human voice? No, that wasn't likely and, anyway, there had been the footprints. Some child - probably a boy - had learned to imitate bird and animal cries and had sneaked up to the caravan in the dark and rain to play a trick on her.

She recalled what Aidan had said about the Pooka, how the plastic bags in which the villagers put dried turf had either been taken or ripped asunder and the sods tossed out on the ground. There had also been trouble with conifers; somebody or something had rooted up saplings which had been planted on the western slope of Slieve Brack. Could there really be a Pooka then - not the mischievous fairy creatures which country people once believed in but a - ? Oh, that was impossible. She would be maintaining next that gossamer was really thread left by the Pooka and that haws turned black in October because he peed on them!

CHAPTER 7

For four suntimes Gerg lurked near the white nest-place, crouching in the heather south of the river whenever Nooma came out. He was terrified that she would spot him and, yet, if he left, the noisy crutins might drive her away. Then it happened. Not long after the fourth sundown lights came bobbing like will-o-the-wisps down the stony path leading to the river. There was something about those yellow beams that caused the hairs on the back of his neck to rise. Moaning nervously he waited.

"Careful, lads!" Johnno gripped the brakes of his mountain bike. It was dangerous whizzing downhill on a boreen when his lamp barely showed the surface.

"Do you think we should walk?" P.J., his mate, shouted.

"No, I don't," Johnno barked. "And keep your voice down."

Next moment there was a slither of tyres, a muttered curse and the clatter of metal on stone.

"All right, lads," Johnno dismounted. "We'll walk from here."

"Freddy, are you hurt?" Gallo called out.

"Never felt better," Freddy picked up his bike. "That is, apart from a crushed knee and a few broken ribs," he added wryly.

"Quiet!" Johnno commanded. "No use letting the Dublin bird know of our visit."

"Suppose she gets frightened?" Miller, the boy who had sided with Aidan in the dispute over the grouse eggs, wheeled his bike alongside Johnno's.

"Yes?" Freddy, who, at ten, was the youngest of the group, chimed in. "She's all on her own."

"We're only going to see how she's getting along," Johnno adjusted the baseball cap covering his bandaged head. "If ye lads are getting cold feet, that's the way home back there."

"But there's no light in the caravan," Miller pointed out. "She must be in bed."

"Then we'll wake her up," Johnno promised. "Maybe she'll come out in the all-together."

The older boys sniggered delightedly at this prospect.

"O'Connor said she's a real babe," Gallo, a well-built thirteen-year-old dressed in black, declared. "He said she has a lovely smile."

"She's probably just a stuck-up cow like all those other city birds," Johnno spoke with the wisdom of his fifteen years. "What does she want, coming down here to live in a bog, anyway? She must be a bit of a nutter."

"Johnno is right," P.J. said. "There was this Dublin bird at the New Year's disco in Fennor and she wouldn't dance with anyone."

"He means she wouldn't dance with him," Gallo whispered to Freddy.

"Quiet!" Johnno hissed.

By this time the group had reached the wooden bridge.

"We'll park the bikes here," Johnno decided. "Then we can creep up without being heard."

Keeping their lamps trained on the ground, the five boys made their way along the boreen to the caravan which showed up ghostly white in the darkness. As they drew near it they switched off their lamps, then silent as shadows in their runners, they felt their way forward. Johnno peered in a window, while P.J. carefully mounted the steps and put his ear to the keyhole. After a minute Johnno mounted the steps also.

"I can see nothing," he whispered.

"She's in there all right," P.J. whispered. "I can hear her breathing."

"Here, let me," Johnno put his own ear to the keyhole. "I can hear nothing," he complained. "You must have -"

He didn't finish. Just then an eerie, drawn-out screech rent the stillness.

"Bloody hell! What's that?" Johnno turned away from the door.

"It could be a barn owl," P.J. backed down the steps, followed by Johnno.

"Did you lads see anything?" Johnno demanded of his huddled followers.

Before anyone could answer, there was a loud splashing sound from the direction of the bridge, followed by another and another.

"Our bikes!" Johnno hissed, racing back along the boreen, a cone of light dancing before him. With the others at his heels, he reached the bridge, panting. Apart from a pair of handlebars sticking out of the water, there was no sign of the bikes.

"Oh, blazes!" P.J. cried. "That bike cost my old fellow seventy quid. He'll kill me."

"Mine cost twice that," Johnno moaned. "And I wouldn't give a damn but I'm supposed to go shooting with Big Jim Burke in the morning."

They shone their lamps back and forth across the surrounding whins and sally trees.

"I'll bet it was that get, O'Connor," Johnno snarled.

"No, it wasn't," Miller spoke in an uneasy voice. "Aidan was going to the pictures with his family."

"He could have said that, then followed us out here," P.J. pointed out.

"He wouldn't tell me a lie," Miller insisted.

"Then who else could have done it?" Johnno demanded. "The Pooka?"

Nobody answered.

"Oh, come on, lads!" Johnno pleaded. "Ye're not going to start that business again."

"You heard the scream," Miller shone his lamp on the brown surface of the river, that looked far more threatening in the dark than it did in daytime.

"Well, I think if it wasn't O'Connor, it was probably the Dublin bird," Johnno tried to project more certainty than he felt. "I believe she wasn't in the caravan at all. Come on, we'll find out."

As the boys strode back along the boreen, the scream that had frightened them before rang out from the other side of the river. At once they came pounding back across the bridge. Tripping and stumbling over the mossy ground in their drenched runners they headed for the area from which the scream had come.

"Look! Over there!" Johnno shouted as his lamp beam picked up a crouching form. The others followed behind him, lamp beams dancing over sedge and heather.

"I can see him," P.J. crowed. "He dodged behind that sally."

"Which one?" three or four voices cried in unison.

"That one!" P.J. charged recklessly. There was an enormous splash accompanied by a choking cry.

While the others stopped to rescue their companion, Johnno continued the chase. They heard him yelping like a hound that has sighted a hare, as they hauled P.J. from the boghole. After P.J.'s clothes had been removed, wrung out and put on again and Gallo had loaned him his jacket, Johnno finally returned.

"What happened?" Freddy asked.

"I don't know," Johnno admitted. "I thought I had him cornered and then he was just gone. I think he must have swum across the river."

"Who was it?" Miller forced himself to ask.

"How should I know?" Johnno snapped. "Probably some joker from Fennor. Are you all right, P.J.?"

"No, I'm not all right!" P.J.'s teeth were chattering. "I'm lucky if I don't catch me death of cold."

"Hurry then," Johnno commanded. "We'll get a few long branches and fish our bikes out of the river."

"This is the last time I'm coming to this lousy bog," P.J.

announced as his companions wrenched branches from a sally tree. "The bloody place is haunted."

As if to confirm what he said, a thin plaintive cry like the scream of a vixen came floating out of the darkness. In spite of themselves the boys shivered.

CHAPTER 8

Maeve walked through the bog, enjoying the glorious sunshine. Everywhere birds were singing and calling: lapwings, skylarks, greycrows, curlews and many more she couldn't recognise. She had even heard the cuckoo! And a hare had gone bounding away from almost under her feet! Oh, it was good to be alive, though during the darkness of night she had vowed she wouldn't spend another day in Eastersnow.

A terrifying screech had awakened her and when she had peeped out the window she had seen a group of shadowy figures just outside. Her heart had almost stopped. And then there had been splashing sounds and the prowlers had run off. Later, she had heard the screech again and then another, fainter cry. She had been too frightened to go back to sleep. What if the prowlers came back? In the morning, tense and bleary-eyed, she had been on the point of walking into Raheen to phone the *gardaí* when Aidan and Eithne had arrived. Their visit had calmed her. They promised that they would report the incident to Big Jim Burke, who would find out who the culprits were.

"Is Big Jim the man who offered £500 for information on the tree vandals?" she asked.

"Yes," Eithne told her. "He's Mr. Hunt's foreman - but you know that, don't you?"

"I suppose I should," Maeve smiled. "My boss, Eileen McGreevy, told me about him but my mind wasn't very clear at the time."

"And do you know Mr. Hunt?" Eithne frowned at Aidan, who was about to pick up the statue of Ganesha.

"Actually, I never set eyes on him," Maeve admitted. "I only know of him through Eileen. Anyway, has nobody claimed the reward?"

"Not yet," Eithne said. "But if any of the fellows in Raheen knew, they would tell him. That's because he pays them to stamp down the grass and weeds choking the young trees."

"They can't tell him because it's not anyone from Raheen who did it," Aidan broke in. "It's the Pooka."

"Or somebody who wants us to believe it's the Pooka," Maeve felt that she could no longer dismiss Aidan's conviction.

After that she had questioned them about the Sweeneys but they had been too young to know much about them. Eithne, however, recalled that Noreen was supposed to be dumb.

"I kind of remember her coming into the shop one day for groceries and handing my mother a list," she waved her hands as if to fan the image into life.

"And what did she look like?" Maeve pressed.

"I'm not sure," Eithne wrinkled her forehead. "Something like you, I guess, except that she kept her eyes on the ground. She looked kind of sad."

Maeve had let the matter drop. When she had tried to pay them for the groceries, they had refused, so she had asked them to tell their father to keep a record of the bills. As soon as she had sold a few paintings she would send Mr. Hunt a money order.

She smiled wistfully. In many ways the O'Connor children reminded her of herself and Danny a long, long time ago - no, she wouldn't let thoughts like that spoil the present. Putting their visit out of her mind, she let her eye range over the varying yellows and duns of moss, peat and heather. The cotton grass was beginning to form white heads and she stopped to pick a bunch. She would place it before the

48

statue of Ganesha. Maybe he would help her to discover who the Pooka was or at least ensure that the prowlers didn't return.

After swimming the river to escape from the noisy crutin with the duck's head, Gerg had scrambled to the nest-cave near the birch tree. Then at first light he had caught a small trout and eaten it on the river bank. Anxious, now, to reach the safety of the Great Hill before the sun rose too high, he set off across the bog at a fast lope.

At a whin-covered bank a cloying odour brought him to a halt. Three fox cubs lay on the freshly dug clay before a den, their skulls crushed, blood oozing from their mouths. Gerg bared his teeth. He had no love for Sionnach's mate, Foomnach, whom he suspected of having murdered Suairc, yet the fluffy corpses roused in him a combination of pity and anger. The crutins had done this, not because they were hungry but because they hated all gagna. Their scent came to him mingled with the ranker scent of dogs. Climbing the bank, he peeped out from behind a whin bush.

Further up the rise a band of crutins with digging irons were approaching the whitethorn in which Babh the Grey Crow and her mate, Balor, had their nest. One of them - was it Lacheen, the noisy crutin whose head covering stuck out in front like a duck's bill? - was carrying something that looked like a fox's tail. The crutin in the lead had a thunder-stick cradled in his arms. From his moustache and great bulk he recognised him as Crumale, and the hairs on the back of his neck stood up. Crumale raised his right hand. The other crutins held the dogs and waited. Forgetting his enmity for Babh and Balor, Gerg cupped his hands about his mouth.

"Stay here, fellows," Big Jim Burke whispered, easing back the safety catch of his shotgun. He started to move slowly towards the whitethorn, in which the crude ball of sticks that was a grey crow's nest showed clearly behind a veil of new leaves. One shot through the side would smash the eggs and kill the hen. He raised the gun butt to his shoulder. Another ten yards and he would be within range. At that instant a warning KRAA! KRAA! sent the hen slipping off the far side of the nest and flapping away.

"Bloody hell!" Big Jim swore, firing both barrels at the retreating Babh.

Out of the side of his eye he caught sight of a brown form ducking behind a whin bush. The Pooka! The bloody little get had mimicked the call of a hoodie. By crikey, he would nail him now! A blast of lead in the backside at sixty yards would put an end to his tricks.

Quickly he broke open his 12-bore, removed the spent cartridges and selecting two No. 5's from his belt, slipped them into the chambers. Then he snapped the gun shut. He had no intention of actually killing the brat but he didn't see how a man could be blamed for nicking him. That September evening two years ago when he had found him lurking near the plantation, he had mistaken him for a deer and let fly with the ·22. He could claim this time that he mistook him for a fox.

Big Jim had good reason to hate the Pooka. When Mr. Hunt heard about the conifers being pulled up he had been furious - a whole season's work put in jeopardy! Then when the same thing had happened again this autumn, he had threatened to sack his foreman. That was when Big Jim had taken the desperate measure of offering £500 of his own money for information. So far nobody had come forward. The question was, WHY? He was very likely one of the village brats, probably that Freddy Moran or that Brian O'Connor — the two were about the same height and build as the Pooka.

His parents thought young O'Connor was a little angel. Some angel! Robbing orchards! Putting bangers through letter boxes at Hallowe'en! Throwing eggs at houses! And he was athletic too, the type that could easily rip up a tree, then take off across country like a hare.

Big Jim signalled to the others to fan out so that they would converge on the whin bush from three sides, leaving only open country for the Pooka's retreat. The men thought he had sighted a fox and obeyed without question, keeping the terrier and mongrels in check. He himself headed casually downhill in a direction that would take him between the whin bush and Harte's culleen, the only cover till one came to Slieve Brack. He stroked his moustache with excitement. The Pooka would rue the day he had first tangled with Big Jim Burke.

CHAPTER 9

Big Jim wasn't the only one who had a score to settle with the Pooka. Johnno was in an ugly mood as he approached the whin bush. The wound on his scalp itched under the baseball cap and he was physically wrecked. It must have been two o'clock by the time they got the last bike out of the river and then they had to cycle home in wet jeans. He was hardly in bed till he had to get up to join Big Jim, who wanted an early start.

Big Jim had come under flak from the gun club for planting evergreens on Slieve Brack; they claimed that he was destroying heather on which grouse fed. That was nonsense because it was vermin and not trees that were to blame for the fall in grouse numbers. If the sportsmen took the trouble to shoot more foxes, magpies and hoodies instead of shooting off their mouths they would have enough grouse to feed an army. Anyway, Big Jim was doing the job for them and Johnno had a good notion why: he was planning to cut down the oaks in Lackendarragh Wood and he didn't want the gun club teaming up with the Green freaks to block him.

Big Jim thought Johnno was nothing but a sap because he preferred to work odd days for him instead of attending Fennor Vocational but Johnno reckoned that school was only for eejits. Even if you got the Leaving Cert you had no guarantee of a job. Johnno meant to get his share of the £500 Big Jim was offering for information on tree vandals - and that meant the Pooka. If they nabbed the Pooka today he expected to get at least a hundred quid for his part. With that stake he could light out for England, where his cousin would get him a start in the buildings.

Stuffing the fox's tail into his pocket so that he could get a proper grip on the handle of his spade, he strode forward. At about the same time Big Jim with a wave of his hand signalled to the men to give the dogs their heads.

Crouching down, Gerg began to race towards Harte's culleen, a narrow glen in which hazels and blackthorns grew. He knew that the dogs would pick up his spoor as soon as they reached the whins. After that it would just be a matter of minutes till they surrounded him. Panting with exertion he increased his speed. The excited yelping of the dogs told that they were giving chase. In another moment he was among the outlying blackthorns - but where could he hide? The dogs would find him, even in the densest thicket. There was only one chance.

Springing frantically he caught the branch of a hazel and swung himself up so that he got a foothold on another branch. There was a bigger tree nearby and he jumped towards it. As he did so he noticed something that gave him renewed heart: a company of stags, ears pricked, were standing in a glade about a stone's throw ahead. Many had shed their antlers.

Gerg always avoided the stags when they were bellowing and fighting during the season of ripe fruit but when they went off in a group by themselves during the seasons of new buds and heather bloom, he walked among them unafraid. Now they stirred nervously, for the clamour of the dogs was growing louder. If they didn't get time to recognise him they might panic. He announced his presence with a gruff bark. They looked up, nostrils drawing in his scent. Would they wait?

Dropping to the ground, he sprinted towards them just as they began to trot. Selecting Caoilte, a stag who had recently lost one of his antlers, he threw himself on his back and buried his fingers in the thick hair of his neck. Caoilte stumbled slightly, then bounded away. Gerg felt his arms almost jerked from their sockets as the stag leaped over rocks, fallen trees and briar clumps. The yelping of the dogs rose to a crescendo; they were now among the trees, sure of their quarry.

When Big Jim saw the dogs give chase, he altered his course so that he would reach the far end of the culleen ahead of them. Racing to a hillock above the dense clusters of hazels and blackthorns, he gritted his teeth with satisfaction. There was no way the Pooka could escape this time.

While he was congratulating himself, five or six stags burst from the trees. To his amazement, something seemed to be clinging to the back of the middle stag, something in rough brown clothes. By the time he had recovered enough to aim, the herd was splashing away towards Slieve Brack with the dogs yapping uselessly behind him.

"No," Big Jim told himself. "It must have been the head of another deer I saw. Yes, that must be it."

As she worked on a view of the bog with Slieve Brack looming in the background, Maeve became more and more tense. Try as she might she couldn't capture the mixture of emptiness and dreamlike serenity which the actual landscape evoked. The colours were darkening into ugly smudges and the luminous simplicity of heather, moss and sky was evading her. If only she hadn't emptied all of her packet into the river … On a Saturday evening like this in Dublin she would be planning a night out with Sean or Damien or Michael, whereas here all she had to look forward to was the possible return of the prowlers.

What would she do if they came back? She was totally isolated, without a phone or a living person within miles. Already the sun was sinking towards the western hills. In a few hours it would be dark! Maybe she should walk into Raheen and ask the O'Connors to put her up for the night? The children would be glad of her company and she could play for them on her recorder. Oh, why had she thrown that packet away?

"Careful, there!" she warned herself. "Don't go down that slippery slope again. Remember where it led in Dublin."

"But I've tried it your way," her other self pointed out, "and it's not working. Why don't you tear up that masterpiece and get a life?"

"I can save it yet," she said. "It's just a matter of the right tones."

"Who are you kidding?" her other self mocked. "You'll no more make it as an artist than you did as a journalist or an employee of GIVE. This hermit business isn't your scene. It might work if you were a Gauguin or a van Gogh but you're just a dabbler. Tear it up and let's party."

Maeve rose from the table and slowly and deliberately tore the water colour into tiny bits.

"Ganesha, you are the god who enables people to overcome obstacles, the god of new beginnings," she addressed his statue out loud. "Help me now to see this through." Ganesha sat with crossed legs on his ivory cushion, his wise elephant gaze fixed in serene contemplation.

She started packing her knapsack. When she was folding her pyjamas, she heard voices. Going to the door, she was surprised to see four boys with bicycles approaching. One of them, a dark-haired handsome fellow, left his bike on the ground and stepped forward.

"We came to apologise, Miss," his voice was rough but manly. "We're the blokes that were here last night. We didn't mean to scare you."

"Oh," she tried to hide her relief. "And why did you decide to apologise?"

"Aidan O'Connor told us that you wanted us reported to Big Jim Burke," the smallest boy piped up. "We made a deal with him that he'd say nothing if we came out here and owned up."

"That's right, Miss," a stocky boy with shoulder length hair confirmed. "We were only messing."

"We didn't think you'd be in bed," a pimply, fair haired fellow with a shaven head added.

"And what are your names?" Maeve had to suppress a smile at their contrite expressions.

"I'm P.J. Durcan," the pimply fellow was taking on the role of spokesman, "and he's Freddy Moran and he's Miller."

"Joe O'Malley," the stocky boy corrected.

"And I'm Charlie Gallagher," the fellow who had spoken first gazed at her with soft, glowing eyes. "My mates call me Gallo."

"Well, you might as well come in since you've come this far," she invited. "I'm afraid, though, I can only offer you orange juice and biscuits."

"Oh, that'll be fine," they assured her, trooping in. They reminded her of Danny when he was a small boy, the way they admired her pictures and accepted their orange juice and biscuits as if it were the greatest treat in the world. By the time they left they regarded her as a friend.

"If you ever need anything, just let me know," Gallo was clearly smitten.

"I will," she promised, watching them cycle off along the rutted boreen.

"All right, Ganesha," she turned away from the door. "I'm going to try that landscape again."

CHAPTER 10

By the time the stags were mounting the uplands to the south of Slieve Brack the dogs had had enough. They broke off the chase and returned with tongues hanging out to their masters. Gerg was too exhilarated by the ride to note their absence. The rise and fall of Caoilte's body no longer jarred him; he was carried along by its surge as a stick is carried by a rushing stream. The wind made his eyes water so that the world was a blur of movement, the brown heather slope of the Great Hill rushing past on one side and the green fields and hedges of Lackendarragh on the other. Below him as he crossed the ridge he could just discern the rounded masses of foliage that marked the oak wood and further south the cloudy line of beeches leading to the great stone nest-place. Down the slope the stags raced, sailing effortlessly over banks and drains, disturbing grazing cattle, plunging through gaps in whitethorn hedges, veering away from a thudding monster tearing up the earth.

At the edge of the wood the stags slowed down and Gerg slid off Caoilte's back. He watched his friends disappear along leafy paths. They would, he knew, make for the upper reaches of the wood, where beneath the mossy boughs of giant oaks they rested during suntime. The hinds and calves born during the last season of cotton bloom kept to the lower part of the wood.

Gerg loved Lackendarragh. In two of the largest oaks he had woven branches into tree-nests, where he dozed on warm suntimes, lulled by the music of the leaves and the soft cooing of pigeons. For a long time there had been no disturbance by crutins. The roof of their great stone nest-place beyond the wood had fallen in and Gerg often slept in a cave beneath the rubble. Now, tired after his narrow escape from Crumale, he headed for this retreat.

Climbing in through a window opening, he made his way into an enclosure formed by ivied walls. Looking up he could see blue sky and a small tree growing from a crack in the stones. There were openings leading to other enclosures surrounding the main one. Satisfied that there was no danger, he picked his way among the rubble heaps and stooping, crawled down into a dry nook lined with withered grass and leaves. Despite the chattering of jackdaws on the wall tops he was soon fast asleep.

When he awoke it was sundown. His stomach rumbled. Sniffing, he located parsnips he had hidden under debris. Any that Francach the Rat hadn't eaten had dried out. He took a bite of one then tossed it aside. Searching, he found his store of hazel nuts. Laying a handful on a stone, he broke the shells with another stone then, morsel by morsel, picked up the crushed kernels. They tasted good but his hunger hadn't abated. Impatiently he covered the remaining nuts with rubble and climbed out through a window opening.

Normally, he didn't venture near farms until star-time, but hunger made him reckless. In a garden behind the nearest crutin nest-place there was a clamp of mangolds he had raided during the last moon season. While he was burrowing in the clay with his hands a strange dog began to bark. Frantically he tore aside the inner layer of rushes covering the mangolds. He heard a door open. In the half light a female crutin called out to the frenzied dog, who came bounding down the garden.

Gerg was tired of being chased by dogs. In the voice of his

old friend Madra he crouched and snarled his anger. He became Madra, fierce and full of power. The charging dog halted, puzzled. Gerg took a handful of clay and threw it in his face. At once the brute retreated to a safer distance then renewed his furious barking. With a mangold in each hand Gerg backed away, snarling all the time. There was a wall behind him. The female crutin was coming down the garden with a thunder-stick. Tossing one of the mangolds into the field, he scrambled over the wall. With the mangold clutched to his side he raced headlong back to the great stone nest-place. There, when he had recovered his breath, he chopped pieces off the mangold with a stone and munched them greedily. Why hadn't the female crutin fired the thunder-stick? Maybe she couldn't see him clearly in the half-light? He would have to avoid her nest-place for some time. Luckily, there were fields of turnips on other farms.

At the next sunup he was aroused by a wild, musical clamour that seemed to fill the entire world outside. Climbing to a window opening he watched a skein of wildgeese flying overhead and he knew that, despite the frost on the ground, the season of dead plants was finally over. Immediately, a longing came on him to join the heather hens on the Great Hill.

After eating the remainder of the mangold, he entered the oakwood, which rang with the voices of chaffinches and pigeons. Most trees were in full leaf but others were just breaking into yellowy green foliage. At a moss-grown giant he heard Keva the Grey Squirrel scolding and climbed up to investigate. As he reached the branches on which the drey was built, Bran the Raven flew out of a nearby tree. Keva had four naked young ones and the presence of Bran had driven her frantic.

While Gerg was purring to the agitated mother, he heard crutin voices. Rising to his full height he saw with a start Crumale and Lacheen further down the wood. Lacheen had a pail like the one in which Nooma brought food to the hens, only smaller, and Crumale had a short stick. Now and then they would halt in front of a tree and Crumale would touch it with the stick. They came to Keva's oak and halted directly under it.

Gerg froze. Without moving his head he could see that the pail contained yellow mud. Crumale dipped the stick in the mud and put some on the bole, chattering all the time to Lacheen, who had on his pointed head covering. Just as they were about to move off, Keva jumped from the drey to a branch, causing leaves to rustle. Gerg held his breath. The two crutins looked up, chattering. Then they moved on. Gerg slowly released his breath.

As soon as the two intruders were out of sight, he climbed down the tree and crept away in the opposite direction. Leaving the oak wood, he made his way by deer trails and sheep paths to the brow of the Great Hill. On the summit there was a cairn in which he had a nest-cave. He would rest there till sundown.

While Gerg was crossing the eastern brow of Slieve Brack, Maeve paused on the lower western slope to admire the mingled colours around her: umber of bracken, yellow of gorse, white of blackthorn, emerald and fawn of grass. Dark green Scots pines grew higher up and, below them, young spruces, looking in the distance like tiny jade Christmas trees, dotted the heather. Delight overcoming her anxiety, she continued her journey.

That morning she had set out to explore the area southeast of the caravan. The sight of Slieve Brack rising so proudly above the plain had tempted her to go higher and higher. It didn't look like a very big mountain - in fact, it probably wasn't a mountain at all - yet, the more she climbed the more the summit seemed to recede. Her legs felt heavy and she wished she had started out much earlier.

A hoarse croak sounded from the Scots pines as she approached them. Presently, a great black crow came sailing out into the open. Could it be a raven? It was certainly the biggest crow she had ever seen. Taking a sloping path through the trees, she noticed, besides the daisies, dandelions and violets, a single white anemone growing among the mosses. How beautiful and fragile it looked! "The Windflower" her mother used to call it. "Look, darling, a windflower!"

Soon she came to the edge of the wood and encountered a wire fence with a drain beneath it. After much searching, she found a gap where she could cross. Parallel to the drain, there was a crumbling stone wall leading up from the valley to the summit and she followed this, though her breath came in short gasps and she occasionally stumbled. Clouds of midges drifted near the trees but they did not bite her.

Deciding that she needed food to restore her strength, she sat on a flat stone and ate the sandwiches she had brought, washing them down with a bottle of water. The view of the valley was magnificent, brown heather merging into a patchwork quilt of green fields and, over to the east, clusters of trees enclosing what appeared to be a Georgian mansion.

On the final stage of the ascent she followed a steep path through the heather and sedge, wondering if she weren't being foolhardy to undertake such a venture on her own. Every step was an effort and she felt that at any moment her lungs might burst. More alarming still, a grey mist was enveloping the summit. What if she lost her way or broke an ankle? If she collapsed up here it might be days before anyone discovered the note she had fastened to the caravan door - by which time she would have died of exposure. Maybe, as it was Sunday, Aidan and Eithne would cycle out ...

As she mounted higher, the mist left the summit and skylarks began to sing overhead. Kok, kok, kok! A dark bird with red wattles over its eyes and a fanned tail rose from the heather and swung down the mountain, crowing. It was just like the one she had seen near the turf clamps. Pressing on, she emerged from the heather into a region of sparse sedge. A hovering kestrel veered off as she gained the crest. About two hundred yards away there was a stone cairn rising dramatically above the bare peat. She trudged towards it, determined not to yield to exhaustion.

CHAPTER 11

The "kee kee kee" of Seabhac the Kestrel woke Gerg. Some enemy was approaching. Swiftly he slipped out of his nest and crept to the upper part of the cairn, where he lay down behind a rock, tensely alert. Presently he saw the head of a crutin rising above the edge of the summit. It was Nooma!

Shivering with excitement, he watched her trudge closer. She was dressed in a blue covering and her brown hair gleamed in the sunlight. How beautiful she was, more beautiful than Gealach the Moon when she rose massive and orange-red above the sleeping mountains!

"Welcome, Nooma," he called in the voice of Donn the Skylark, then when he saw her eye scanning the cairn, he backed away and easing himself down the far side, scampered off across the moss and sedge. Reaching a shallow depression in the peat, he threw himself down, ignoring the oozing brown water. How did she find out he was sleeping here? Had she come to lock him up in her white nest-place?

The view from the top of the cairn amply repaid Maeve's exertions: on one side lay the valley of Eastersnow and on the other the blue mountains. She saw that Eastersnow River flowed out of a lake in which there were two islands, the larger one wooded. The lake was hardly more than a mile from her caravan.

Turning her attention to the cairn, she noticed that it contained a number of partly opened chambers or recesses. Could this have been a Stone Age burial site? Maybe St. Nuadhan had come here to fast and pray as St. Patrick had done on Croagh Patrick? She ventured into one of the recesses. To her amazement she found a nest made of heather and lined with a torn potato sack and moss. Surely no bird, not even an eagle, would have made so huge a nest? Gingerly she touched the moss and sack with her hand. Was it her imagination that told her they felt warm?

Going on her hands and knees, she searched the entire recess. Behind a flat stone in one corner there were hazel nut shells and what looked like a gnawed turnip stump. Could a squirrel have brought them here? The image of the wet potato sack hanging in Jimmy Mac Dermott's byre flashed into her mind - oh no!

Troubled, she left and explored the other recesses. They were all empty. She wanted to examine the first one again but it was growing late. Suppose a mist descended? And even if one didn't, she had to get down from the mountain and across the bog before darkness. Hastily she climbed up to the cairn's rim.

Gerg had not long to wait before he saw Nooma crossing the cairn, holding out both arms to keep her balance. She disappeared from view and he guessed that she was exploring his nest-cave. He called out to her in the voice of Plibeen the Lapwing and Naoscach the Snipe but if she heard, there was no response. For ages he lay in the cold water, caught between the desire to venture close and watch her and the desire to flee back to Lackendarragh.

When he felt he could endure his predicament no longer, she mounted the far rim of the cairn. As soon as she had descended below his line of vision, he crept back and climbed the cairn on all fours. She wasn't in sight. Rising, he hurried across the sunken interior, hopping from stone to massive stone. When he peeped out over the rim, she was already a hundred paces away.

He was about to follow at a distance, when he saw her waving to somebody further down. Immediately he froze. Nooma had halted too, waiting. After a short time two brightly clothed young crutins, one with short brown hair, the other with long dark hair, came rising into view and hurried towards her. The three stood there chattering in their own tongue. He had never heard Nooma chatter before and pain seared through his mind. He wasn't her only young one; these were hers also. That was why she hadn't wanted him. That was why she had locked him away in the hens' nest-place.

The journey down the mountain, while easier, was not without incident. Maeve slipped twice on wet moss and hurt her toes. Nevertheless, they all arrived at the bottom in one piece and set off for the caravan, Aidan chattering away, Eithne graver and more guarded. They didn't know what the cairn was but Aidan thought it might be a fairy fort.

"You mean a ring fort," Eithne corrected. "And the ring fort is somewhere up there in those pines."

When Maeve described the bird that had risen crowing out of the heather, Aidan declared it was a cock grouse. He also told her about Big Jim Burke's encounter with the Pooka and how the Pooka had escaped on a stag's back.

"You shouldn't listen to Johnny O'Rourke's tall stories," Eithne admonished.

"It's not a tall story," Aidan insisted. "Johnno was there when it happened."

"Oh, yeah!" Eithne rolled her eyes.

"In that case, what happened to the brown creature the dogs were chasing?" Aidan demanded. "Tell me that, Miss Know-all."

"I'm sure I don't know," Eithne tossed her head.

"Do you believe in fairies, Aidan?" Maeve couldn't help asking.

"No, I don't," Aidan said. "But goblins are funny and I do believe in the Pooka."

"That's because you believe everything Jimmy Mac Dermott told you," Eithne remarked.

"Well, didn't Jimmy leave out a saucer of milk for him every night?" Aidan's voice rose. "And in the morning it was always gone."

"Cats," Eithne scoffed.

Maeve was tempted to tell them about what she had found in the cairn but she hesitated. Suppose Aidan let it slip and it came to the ears of Big Jim Burke? If he was capable of shooting at the Pooka then the less he knew of his probable whereabouts the better.

"Where is Jimmy Mac Dermott now?" she asked to ease the tension.

"Above in the Nursing Home," Eithne told her.

"I wish I could meet him," Maeve looked thoughtful. "I'm sure he could tell me a lot about this mysterious creature."

Gerg watched till the three crutins disappeared below the brow of the mountain then he dragged himself back to the nest-cave. Nooma's scent hung in the air like the scent of bog myrtle. Without removing his sack he sat on the floor and folding his arms about his knees, began to rock himself back and forth. The wet sack chafed his skin, so he decided to remove it and put on the one in the nest. When he lifted up the other sack there was a faint tinkle. An object on the floor caught his eye, a silvery thing in the shape of two crossed twigs with a loop on top. Trembling he picked up the object. He turned it over and raised it to his nose. Nooma must have dropped it: her scent was on it. He held it in his palm as if it were an icicle that might suddenly dissolve. He pressed it to his bare chest, enjoying its coldness. He was filled with awe. It was the most wondrous thing he had ever seen. He felt like he did that first time when he had lifted Suairceen out of the crevasse and she had rested cheeping in his hand. What should he do with it?

Even as the question occurred to him, he knew the answer. He would bring it to the white nest-place. Nooma would find it at sunup and realise that Gerg too was her young one.

CHAPTER 12

That night as she undressed, Maeve discovered that her ankh was missing. She searched the caravan but didn't find it. What should she do now? Pray to St. Anthony as her mother would have done? Invoke Ganesha? She wouldn't mind but it was a present from Michael Vaughan. Michael was her best friend in the Green movement. Actually, he was more than a friend - or would be if she hadn't told him off for criticising her life-style. She told him that she had had enough lectures from her parents, that he wasn't her father. She accused him of being a ruthless newshound who wouldn't let anything get in the way of his career.

Of course she was being over-the-top but then in Dublin she was often like that. Michael had his virtues and one of them was calling a spade a spade. That was why she wore his ankh instead of her old wooden one. It was a reminder that if she wanted his respect she would have to earn it - no more trips on the drug roller coaster. Of course it was easier said than done. That was why she had to get out of Dublin. And now she had lost the ankh.

Where could it have fallen off the chain? When she slipped coming down the mountain? When she had searched the recess on her hands and knees? She regretted that she hadn't taken the children into her confidence; if they had gone back to look at the nest they might have found the ankh. She would have to go back herself in the morning.

Once her head rested on the pillow she fell into an exhausted sleep in which she dreamed that the Pooka was singing to her in all the diverse voices of the wilderness, now sad, now challenging, now appealing. She tossed and turned but did not wake up. When she opened the door in the morning she saw on the top step a little nest made of heather and moss. Her ankh was lying inside.

Leaving the nest on the doorstep, Gerg turned sadly away. He had sung to Nooma from the glowing of the first stars to the drowning of Gealach the Moon in a lake of cloud but she had not come out. If he waited for Grian the Sun to rise, she would be able to see him. Suppose she didn't like him? She might lock him up or she might turn him over to Crumale, who would certainly kill him. He would go back to the Great Hill, to Tuan and Fand the Heather Fowl, who would not ignore him.

Crossing the river by the bridge, he turned back towards the high ground, walking carefully because of the darkness. In a place where the crutins had torn peat from under the surface of the bog he stumbled repeatedly. Would they do the same again during the next season of cotton bloom? If they did he would tear up their bright shiny peat sacks and scatter the peat.

After some time Gealach reappeared and Gerg broke into a lope that carried him swiftly through sedge and heather, past whin and boulder, up towards the looming bulk of the Great Hill. Before entering the wood, he turned his face to the sky. Why did Gealach change? On this particular star-time all of her face was darkened, except for one yellow edge. He knew that in time she would, as was her way, grow to full brightness again but he felt much evil would happen before then. There was danger in the air - and, yet, she was the Bright One. Could Nooma be like her, able to change from brightness to darkness and back again to brightness?

He furrowed his brow, unable to answer the question. Somewhere in the vast cavern of the sky, Plibeen the Lapwing was mewing, calling out to him. He cupped his hands round his mouth and mewed a response, a great, wavering cry of loneliness that floated over the shadowy emptiness of the bog. Gealach watched, unmoved by his plight.

Turning away, he slunk into the dark recesses of the woods. There in a nest-cave that centuries before had been the storage tunnel of a ring fort and more recently the sett of a badger, he curled up and slept. He spent the next sunup foraging for roots and flower heads and when he came upon the nest of Snag the Magpie in a tall Scots pine, he ate the eggs, for Snag was a thief and a killer of grouse chicks.

From his branch in the pine he watched sheep grazing the heather on the southern slope of the Great Hill, Goll the Grey Crow searching for unguarded nests and Giorria the Hare bounding into his form in a mossy hummock. He knew that Tuan and Fand were out there but he did not want to approach them till dusk for fear of giving away the position of their nest.

As if in confirmation of this risk, a hush descended on the mountain. The larks and the pipits stopped singing and the only sounds were the tinkling of water in a distant stream and the sighing of the breeze through the pine needles. Gerg scanned ground and sky for the cause of the hush and quickly found it: Maar the Peregrine Falcon was circling over the southern slope of the Great Hill. Even as he watched, Maar stooped. Gerg's heart jumped with fright: a dark bird was whirring across the heather right in the path of the diving falcon. It was Tuan!

At the very moment that Maar, talons outstretched, was about to strike, Tuan jinked. Maar overshot her target but she quickly recovered, swung around in mid-air and sped after the retreating Tuan. Fast and furiously the two skimmed the slope, heading towards Lackendarragh. Gerg could see Tuan's wings beating so rapidly they became a blur, then held fixed while he glided downhill like a shooting star. But Maar would not give up.

"Gobak, Gobak, Gobak!" Gerg crowed, noticing a rusty wire fence directly in Tuan's path. But Tuan must have seen it too because, unexpectedly, he veered through a hole near the top. Maar only escaped instant death by banking. That was enough for the falcon. She broke off the chase and flew slowly off towards the mountains, while Tuan disappeared from view around the shoulder of the Great Hill.

Gerg recalled the feeling he had while watching Gealach, that there was danger in the air. Could the danger have been Maar and was it now over? He did not think so. For some reason his unease persisted. At dusk he crept through the heather, calling softly to Tuan, but after being chased by Maar, Tuan was nervous and would not venture near him. Gerg understood but, nevertheless, his heart was heavy. He wished that Suairceen were still alive. Early next sunup he departed for Lackendarragh.

Maeve gazed at the nest with a mixture of awe and delight. It was like the time she had won first prize in the RTE art competition: the postman had come with an enormous parcel and she had been afraid to open it till her mother told her not to be silly. Then she had torn off the wrapper and there had been a fabulous painting set inside, with tubes of paint and a canvas board. She mustn't have been dreaming then during the night when she thought she heard singing; the Pooka - or the creature or whatever it was - had been outside just as on the first night she arrived. And he had left this present.

She was even more touched than she had been when Michael gave her the ankh on the anniversary of their first meeting. How much thought must have gone into shaping this nest! It reminded her of something Danny used to make out of odds and ends and proudly present to their mother. But she would have to get a hold on herself. It could still be a trick. Suppose Aidan had found the ankh and decided to use it to convince her there was really a Pooka? Oh, no! He didn't seem that sort. That meant that whoever left it was the same creature - no, person - who had sung to her before ...

But how could she win his trust so that he wouldn't run away when he saw her? Should she go back to the cairn and leave food or a sack for him? That would be the best move, if she weren't so exhausted. All of her muscles ached and her toes still hurt. She would go as soon as she felt up to it. In the meantime, if she could only talk to Jimmy Mac Dermott ... Maybe, after breakfast, she should try hitching a lift into Raheen so that she could arrange for a taxi to the Nursing Home ...

CHAPTER 13

Before he was halfway to Lackendarragh, Gerg heard the noise, a whining, snarling sound like no sound he had ever heard before. The noise died down then started up again and rose to a crescendo, spluttered out then rose again, humming, grating, jarring. Suddenly there was silence followed by a tremendous crash, as if a thunderbolt had struck the wood. Gerg cowered in terror while pigeons rose clattering out of the oak tops and the distant alarm calls of blackbirds and thrushes floated towards him.

Soon the noise recommenced, rising and falling, growing so shrill it almost pierced his head then dying down to a continuous hum or stopping unexpectedly. After a while the whining was counterpointed by the growling of a thudding monster and he knew that there were crutins in the wood. Should he go back to the Great Hill? No, he decided. He would have to find out what was happening. He would hide near the great stone nest-place till the crutins left then he would venture out.

As the Volkswagen pulled up before the Nursing Home, Maeve began to feel apprehensive. Since Wednesday was a half-day in the shop, Mr. O'Connor had insisted on driving her to Fennor. What was the point in wasting money on a taxi when he could drop her off, then take care of some business himself?

"I'll be back in half an hour," he promised, speeding away with a friendly wave of his hand.

Maeve checked that she had the present of tobacco in her pocket then, drawing a deep breath, she pushed in the heavy door.

"This is it," she told herself. "You can't chicken-out now."

Once she had got directions from a brusque nurse and walked past rooms where old women sat by their beds with vacant faces, her gloom deepened. It required an effort not to turn on her heel and run blindly from the building. And, yet, she couldn't let this chalice pass ... It was in a place like this that her own mother had spent her final year ... her mother, whom she had cursed and told to shut up every time she had tried to make friends with her. What devil had possessed her that she had acted so cruelly? Of course, she was only a teenager then, a rebel determined to go her own way, no matter whom she hurt.

"Forgive me, Mamma," she whispered, pausing by a window to stop herself from collapsing. "I'm sorry I wouldn't let you speak to me. I was blinded with anger and resentment - but I loved you, Mamma. I did. And if I have to live as a hermit for the rest of my life to prove it -"

"Are you all right, Miss?" a young nurse with a ruddy complexion and a warm, country accent laid her hand on her arm.

"Oh, yes, thank you," she smiled apologetically. "I just felt faint for a moment. Can you show me where Jimmy Mac Dermott's room is?"

"Indeed, I can," the nurse's eyes twinkled. "Are you a relation of his?" When Maeve shook her head, she added, "Jimmy is a real character. We all have a soft spot for him."

"I'm living in a caravan near his home," Maeve felt she should explain. "I just thought he might like a visitor."

"They all do," the nurse gave her an approving smile. "It breaks the monotony. Come with me."

They walked down a long corridor until they came to a recreation room partially filled with men listlessly playing draughts, watching television or chatting by the fire.

"Stay here, Miss, and I'll bring him out to you," the nurse instructed.

Jimmy, a weather beaten man with wiry grey hair and a roguish glint in his eye, was at first puzzled to find he had a visitor.

"Do I know you, Miss?" he enquired.

"No," she confessed and introduced herself.

"Well, glory be!" he exclaimed. "And you're living in Eastersnow! Now, isn't that something?"

She offered him the tobacco and he accepted it with feigned reluctance.

"I'm encouraging your bad habits," she joked.

"Arragh, not at all!" he took out a blackened pipe and started to fill it from the packet. "No matter what the doctors say, the smoking never did me any harm. Many a time when I was alone in the house of a winter's night and not another soul within miles, it was the only company I had."

"Except for the Pooka?" she saw him wince.

"So you saw him too?" he paused in the act of striking a match.

"No," she admitted, "but I heard him," and she recounted everything that had happened, including the finding of the nest in the cairn.

"Fair dues to you, Miss, but you're a brave one to stay out there on your own," he struck a match. "At least I had the shotgun."

"You didn't fire at him, did you?" there was indignation in her voice. "After all, apart from pulling up the trees and making off with the turf bags, he hasn't harmed anyone."

Jimmy puffed thoughtfully at his pipe before answering. "There never was a truer word," he agreed, "but when I saw him staring in the window at me and the ugly gob on him like a devil out of hell, it put the heart crossways in me. 'Damn me', said I to myself, 'I won't be terrorised in my own house,' and I out and let fly at him."

"What exactly did he look like?" Maeve tried to contain her eagerness.

"Oh, like a young gossoon of eight or nine that you'd roll in muck. He had matted glibs of hair hanging down to his shoulders and bulging eyes that would remind you of a rabbit caught in a trap or a frightened hare."

"Then he is human?"

"Sure how could he be human and him living out in the bog like a snipe or a curlew? No, he was some sort of fairy - that or a devil."

"Oh, come now, Jimmy," she used his first name to soften the criticism, "surely you don't expect me to believe that you regard the fairies as real?"

"Ah, there's no pulling the wool over your eyes, Miss," he smiled approvingly, then his expression grew troubled. "But if he isn't a fairy, what on earth is he? Answer me that."

"I can't," she confessed. "Maybe he's a child that was reared by animals - foxes or badgers? But that's not very likely - though there are stories of wolf children - and he didn't make human sounds ... Jimmy, there was a family living near you - the Sweeneys wasn't it?"

"Joe Sweeney and his granddaughter, Noreen. God rest their souls. Oh, that was a terrible tragedy - both of them burnt alive! I blame myself for not having noticed the smoke sooner - but, sure, how could I and it all happening during the night? It was Ben that woke me with his whining. It couldn't have been more than five o'clock in the morning. When I got there the house was already an inferno. God have mercy on them both ..."

Noticing his distress, Maeve hesitated before continuing: "You mentioned your dog. How did he react to the Pooka?"

"Faith, that was the strangest thing," Jimmy removed his pipe from his mouth and tamped the half burned tobacco with his finger, "he never barked when he was around the place and if a fox or a stranger came within a mile of the house, he'd raise the roof."

Their conversation was interrupted by an anxious looking man who shuffled up to tell Jimmy that it was time for their tea.

"Don't worry, Paddy," Jimmy patted his arm. "I'll be along in a minute."

"Oh, I'm keeping you from your tea," Maeve said apologetically.

"Not at all, Miss," Jimmy assured her. "That poor devil has

a demon of gluttony in him; he's always worrying about meals."

With a stab of guilt Maeve recalled her father's insistence on punctuality at mealtimes. Poor Dad ... so set in his ways ... God have mercy on him.

"I'll just ask you one more question," she felt like Silvia pumping an informant. "Could it have been the Pooka that set Sweeney's house on fire?"

"You have me there, Miss," Jimmy tapped his pipe against a radiator to remove the ashes, "It was just after that time that he began haunting me. Still, apart from taking eggs and turnips, he did no serious damage."

CHAPTER 14

It was sundown when the crutins left. Gerg heard their droning chariots passing the great stone nest-place and when they had disappeared down the line of beech trees, he hurried to the wood. Guided by the aroma of oozing sap, he emerged into an unexpected opening. The scene of destruction that met his eyes was numbing: Keva's oak was lying prostrate, some of its boughs fractured, others half buried in the ground, their pale green leaves already wilting. But it was the scenes of hidden destruction that affected him most: the burrow of Kuineen the Rabbit smashed in; bright blue egg shells by Smolach the Thrush's broken nest; Keva's drey scattered among the ferns, her four naked babies dead ...

"I shouldn't have left them," Gerg told himself. "I should have known that Crumale and Lacheen were going to harm them when they put yellow mud on the bole."

He hurried on, trying to escape the horror of what he had seen. In a little while he came to another opening where a tree had stood. This giant had been dismembered, the limbs pushed into heaps, the smaller branches scattered in a wide leafy circle. The trunk lay on the broken earth, one end touching the rooted stump, the other resting on a nest of sawdust. It was hard to imagine how proud and alive this tree had been a few suntimes ago. Now it was no longer a tree; it was just an ugly jumble in the wood.

Anger began to replace his shock. Why did the crutins do these things? Why did they hate the bog and the tree and gagna? A shift in the breeze carried a smell like the stench of putrid flesh to his nostrils and he knew that one of their growling monsters was near. He sped down a path of crushed undergrowth, the smell getting stronger and stronger.

Presently, he came to a third opening, with a dead giant half filling it. In the wan light the monster of the crutins rested by the edge of the opening. There was something about its angular, yellow bulk which set it apart from the world of living green behind it, an alien presence. Was it waiting for sunup so that it could continue its work of destruction?

His anger boiled up, blind, intoxicating. Seizing a heavy, mossy stone in both hands, he rushed forward. Instantly, the wood rang with the clanging of metal, the screeching of blackbirds, the cracking of glass, the clattering of pigeons' wings.

Only when tiredness overcame him did he limp away, his foot bleeding from a cut he had got by stepping on broken glass. Reaching the great stone nest-place, he climbed in by the window opening, unaware that he had left a bloody footprint on the sill. Slowly he made his way to his nest and pressing moss that he had brought with him on his wound, bound it in place with ivy stems. Then satisfied that the bleeding had stopped, he curled up and fell fast asleep.

He awoke with a start. There was the crunch of heavy boots in the passage. He began to crawl towards his bolt hole, the cut foot sending pain shooting up his leg. On peeping out he saw that two crutins with heavy sticks were blocking both window openings. One of them was Lacheen. Crumale's voice resounded behind him - he must have discovered the nest! There was only one hope for him: he would have to climb the ivy covered wall and escape through an upper window opening.

A shout from Lacheen told him he had been spotted. At once he began to cross the rubble, hobbling with the pain in his foot. He was halfway up the ivy when Lacheen grabbed his ankle and yanked him down, screaming. Falling on his hands, he struggled to rise but something crashed against the back of his head. There was a blinding crimson flash, then darkness.

He came to in a stone nest-place with musty straw on the floor. His head ached and when he moved it, a feeling of nausea engulfed him. From the pain in his wrists and ankles he knew they were tied. The only light came through a space under the door but to judge from the smells, the place had been used to store digging irons and potatoes.

A rat came out of a corner and began to slink along the wall. Gerg yikkered angrily, sending it scurrying back to its hole. Like his friends, the heather hens, he regarded the Frankee, or rat tribe, as murderous thieves. If there were more of them nearby, they would come and attack him. Twisting gently he tried to turn over on his back but the nausea returned and he stopped.

What would he do now? Even in the hens' nest-place he had not been tied up. It was likely that Crumale intended to kill him. Fear gnawed at his mind. He would never roam the countryside again, never climb the slopes of the Great Hill and watch with Tuan and Fand the bees foraging in the heather and the swallows weaving and looping overhead. Frantically he tugged at the cords binding him till his wrists and shins were raw. Then he lay still, whimpering, remembering Suairc and Nooma.

Big Jim Burke was in a quandary: he had victory within his grasp and yet, everything could still come to nothing. Hadn't his mother often reminded him that, "There's many a slip between the cup and lip"? The trouble had begun when he phoned Mr. Hunt's Dublin office, only to be told by his secretary that he was out of the country. Of all the damn luck! He had finally captured the Pooka but instead of getting thanks, he was being handed a can of worms. For one thing there was the problem of what to do with the damn creature: was he to be treated as an animal or a human? If the latter, then Big Jim could be in trouble with the law - no matter that the imp had just done almost six hundred pounds worth of damage to a JCB. He could picture some furious judge sentencing him to Mountjoy for grievous bodily assault and wrongful imprisonment of a minor.

And what if the Pooka died? There was always the chance that he had been concussed by the blow on the head - a blow that he had struck. It would be only elementary common sense to bring a doctor to him but that could mean the whole thing getting into the papers, and if there was one thing Mr. Hunt didn't want - especially now that the Lackendarragh project was going ahead - it was publicity. Big Jim would have to make sure that the Pooka was alive and well when Mr. Hunt returned. After that, matters would be out of his hands.

Taking Johnny O'Rourke with him in his Land Cruiser, Big Jim drove back that evening to Lackendarragh. Behind the gatehouse, they approached a shed which had been fitted with a new padlock. After listening for sounds from inside, Big Jim opened the door slightly and peeped in. The huddled figure on the floor didn't move. Leaving Johnno, who was armed with an axe handle, to guard the door, Big Jim stepped warily across the straw covered flags. In the dim light he could see the matted hair and the thin, naked, brown arms bound behind the Pooka's back.

"We're here to help you, boy, not to hurt you," he tried to make his voice gentle. "Look, I've food and medicine in this bag. Easy now, boy, while I feel your pulse. There now, easy … Well, you're alive, anyway. Now I'm going to - Bloody hell! The bastard tried to bite me! Easy. I'm just going to dab disinfectant on your head. Ouch! If you try that again, by crikey, I'll flatten you. Here, Johnno, you dab it on his foot while I hold him … There now, that wasn't too bad, was it? How does the foot look, Johnno?"

"I think it's okay," Johnno said. "But I can't be sure in this light. I'll put a Band-aid on it. He stinks like a fox!" he added when the job was done.

"Get back to the door," Big Jim still kept his knee on the wiry, sack-covered back. "Now, Pooka, don't be afraid. I'm only going to cut your hands free. There!"

He rose and stepped back swiftly, as the boy watched him with fierce, distrustful eyes. "Food," he took sandwiches from a brown paper bag and ate one with much lip smacking to show it was tasty. "And this is water," he drank from a large plastic container. "Yum!" he exclaimed, rubbing his stomach with feigned satisfaction. The boy's expression did not change.

Big Jim left the food on the straw. "Now, Johnno," he locked the door behind him and turned to his helper, "dab some of that disinfectant on my finger."

Gerg waited till Crumale and Lacheen left, then, ignoring the pain in the back of his head, he dragged himself forward and turning over, sat up. Raising the plastic container to his mouth, he drank greedily. Never had water tasted so delicious; it was better than dripping ice, better than bilberry juice, better than rain on his tongue. Thirst satisfied, he put down the container and began to pry at the cords binding his ankles. The knots were too tight so he paused to regain his strength.

He was about to resume his attempt when, the smell of the sandwiches proving irresistible, he opened one, sniffed the unfamiliar meat and butter inside, then took a bite. The taste was bland but pleasant. Reassured, he wolfed sandwich after sandwich till there were only two left. He drank some more water and belched. Now he turned his attention once more to the knots, attacking them frantically with his strong nails. After a while the top one gave, then the next. In a few moments he was free.

Gently he massaged his ankles. The pain made him wince but gradually it subsided and he was able to rise to his feet. Undeterred by the pins and needles in his toes, he limped to the door and listened. There was no sound, except for the rustle of insects and the occasional squeak of a bat. He pushed at the door; it did not give. Dropping to his knees, he slipped his fingers under the stout planks and tugged. There was the grating of metal on metal but almost no movement. Bending, he sniffed at the opening; no fresh odour of crutin tainted the air. So Crumale had not bothered to stay on guard! That meant that he believed Gerg couldn't escape. But he had escaped once before, and from a nest-place something like this.

Reaching up, he felt for the top of the wall; it was further up. Since his foot was sore and the lump on the back of his head still ached, he couldn't risk jumping. He groped his way around the walls. They were all solid to the touch. The long walls were five paces and one and the short walls five paces less one. Returning to the door, he threw his weight against it. Immediately, a wave of dizziness swept over him. Sinking to the floor, he decided to rest. A rustle in the straw told him Francach the Rat was approaching.

"Gobak! Gobak!" he crowed. Francach did not budge so Gerg hissed like Dobarchu the Otter. Immediately Francach slunk off but knowing he would return, Gerg threw bread into the corner where he had disappeared. After that he curled up in the straw and fell asleep.

CHAPTER 15

"How did the visit go?" Mr. O'Connor started the engine as soon as Maeve opened the car door.

"Great!" she sat down in the passenger seat. "They're having their tea now or I would have stayed longer. We were just getting to the nitty gritty when the nurse came."

"It's just as well," Mr. O'Connor laughed, "or I would have missed my own supper." He was a jolly man with a pink face and a sandy coloured toupee to cover his bald crown.

"Oh, I am sorry," Maeve apologised. "I never realised that I was staying so long. It's just that Jimmy is such a fascinating person."

"Don't I know," Mr. O'Connor agreed, driving off. "Did he tell you all about the Pooka?"

"Yes," she fastened her seat belt, "but I didn't have time to get all the information about his neighbours. Anyway, I'm to visit him again. He made me promise."

"When you say 'his neighbours', do you mean the Sweeneys?" Mr. O'Connor's voice was suddenly grave.

"Yes," Maeve replied. "It must have been a terrible shock for everybody."

"It was that," Mr. O'Connor sounded as if he were on the point of crying. "You should have seen the granddaughter, Noreen, when she first came to Eastersnow - the loveliest girl you'd see in a month of Sundays. She had a tragic background - both her parents and her young brother were killed in a car accident. She was the only one that came out of it alive and then -" he broke off, struggling to regain his composure.

She was almost like me then, Maeve realised with a start: Mam and Dad dead and Danny in Australia. But she wasn't responsible for the accident, while I - No! No!

"Anyway," Mr. O'Connor continued, "Joe decided to look

after her, though it was a lonesome spot for a young girl used to the city - her family lived in Galway. But I suppose she was fond of the grandfather and he doted on her. You'd hear her singing like a skylark as she helped him drive in the goat or clamp the turf, and when she came into mass on Sunday the whole chapel couldn't take their eyes off the pair of them. Oh, she was as bright and airy as an angel, with glossy black curls and laughing eyes. And then she changed. Whatever happened to her, she lost the power of speech and she became withdrawn. You wouldn't think that the poor, downcast creature that used to come into the shop for groceries was the same girl that used to have us all smiling just to see her. You know, Maeve, it's a horrible thing to say, but I sometimes think it was best how it all ended. What would have become of a poor dumb creature like that once the grandfather died? She would have ended up like a hermit, with nobody to - Oh, forgive me. I'm after putting my big foot in it! Not that I'm implying there's anything wrong with living on your own, but - well, you know what I mean?"

"I know," she assured him. "It's one thing to choose a certain way of life, another to have it forced on you by circumstances. But tell me this, what age was Noreen when she became dumb?"

"Well, now, let me see," Mr. O'Connor bit his lower lip. "I'd say she was about fifteen or sixteen. She must have been about seven when she came to live with Joe and she was eight or nine years with him - Yes, that's right because she had left school about a year when it happened."

"Did she leave school before she was sixteen then?" Maeve wasn't sure when sixteen became the legal school-leaving age.

"Now that you ask, I think she could have left at fourteen," Mr. O'Connor accelerated past a man driving a tractor. "I remember the wife commenting on it at the time. She was attending the convent in Fennor and you'd think the nuns would have complained. But I suppose they reckoned there was no one else to look after the grandfather. Anyway,

84

nobody reported her to the guards that I know of."

"So she wouldn't have done her Junior Cert?" Maeve wanted to establish the facts.

"I doubt it," Mr. O'Connor said. "She would have been too young. Not that she wouldn't be capable of doing it. She was an intelligent girl."

"And how long ago was the fire?" Maeve asked.

"It will be six years exactly on the Twenty Fifth of this month," Mr. O'Connor declared triumphantly. "I remember the date because it was just after the third birthday of our younger lad, Brian - he was born on the Twenty Fourth of May. She was about twenty-one then, just a few months younger than yourself. May she rest in peace."

"Amen," Maeve murmured, lost in thought. "There's something that just occurred to me," she added. "Does anybody have any idea why she changed?" Even as she asked the question she recalled that it was at the age of sixteen she herself had changed from a relatively quiet girl into a raging devil, who cursed and defied her parents.

"Oh, there was plenty of talk," Mr. O'Connor hesitated. "Some of it, as you can imagine, wasn't very nice. Most people thought it had something to do with the car accident, that she had shut it out of her mind and then something or other brought it all back. But quite a few people thought it was because of something that happened to her in Eastersnow - some bad thing. You know what I'm getting at?"

"Yes, I think I do," she realised that it would embarrass him to pursue the matter further so she switched the conversation back to her visit, telling him how Jimmy had hinted that he might sign over his house to her.

"He really must have taken a shine to you!" Mr. O'Connor laughed. "Do you know he refused thirty thousand for that place before he went to the Nursing Home?"

"You're not serious?" she did not have to feign surprise. "Who would give thirty thousand for a run-down house and a few acres of bog?"

"Somebody you know," he prompted.

"Mr. Hunt?" she said and watched him nod. "But what use would it be to him?"

"Oh, plenty of use," he assured her. "Mr. Hunt plans to buy up all of the valley north of the river as far as Loch Glin and to plant it with trees. Forestry is the big money spinner now."

Maeve did not sleep well that night. The dead girl's image kept revolving in her mind so that sometimes she herself was in the car crash or working in the bog with her grandfather or walking with him to mass on Sunday, then a door would clang shut, blotting out the sunlight, and she would find herself falling down and down into bottomless destruction.

She was grateful, when she awoke, for the familiar daylight, grateful to hear the bubbling calls of curlews and the twittering of newly arrived swallows as they chased flies above the river. Rising, she thanked God for the beauty of his creation, then she prepared her frugal breakfast.

"Yoo hoo!" Aidan's voice brought her to the door of the caravan. He and Eithne were pedalling furiously along the rutted boreen. They jumped off their bikes and threw them on the ground.

"Miss," Aidan cried, rushing up to her, "we have fantastic news for you. Jim Burke caught the Pooka!"

"He's holding him in a shed at Lackendarragh!" Eithne was just as excited as her brother.

"Easy now, children," Maeve tried to remain calm. "Are you quite certain?"

"Yes," Eithne panted. "Joe O'Malley swore it's true. He heard Johnno telling P.J. Durcan. Johnno was there when they captured him yesterday morning. He said he's just about the size of our Brian - who's just up to my shoulder."

"He has brown skin and long, matted hair," Aidan broke in. "And he smells like a fox."

"Joe made us promise not to tell anybody," Eithne continued, "and we won't, except you."

In the first light Gerg saw that the roof was made of iron and his heart sank. Once again he was locked in, trapped.

Frantically he threw himself against the door, hitting it again and again till his shoulder hurt. He lay on the straw and looked with one eye through the space under the door. He could see blades of grass and a dandelion. The grunting of Duach the Badger came to him and he grunted in turn, begging Duach to help him. At long last Duach came shuffling up but he was in an irritable mood. He sniffed under the door at Gerg's face, scratched half-heartedly at the stones, then turned away.

Gerg watched his grey form disappear among the shining green grass and tears welled in his eyes. He was all alone now, his only company Francach, who was attempting to steal his remaining food. "Gobak, gobak, gobak!" he crowed shrilly.

Eyeing him defiantly Francach retreated to his hole. Gerg limped to a corner, sat down, and clasping his hands about his knees, began to rock himself to and fro, whimpering.

"Nooma! Nooma!" his heart cried. "Nooma! Nooma!"

CHAPTER 16

Maeve was in a dilemma: her heart told her that she should act at once to free the Pooka but her mind told her to be cautious, to weigh up the consequences of such action. Suppose it was the Pooka that had set Sweeneys' house on fire? He had pulled up young trees and done extensive damage to a JCB, so he was obviously capable of vandalism. Would she not be better to put him out of her mind? After all, she had come to Eastersnow to work as an artist, not to become the champion of some half-beast child. Then she recalled how this child had returned her ankh and sung to her on her first night in the caravan - no, cried out to her like a lost soul. Could she now turn her back on him?

Even as she asked herself the question, the image of her brother, Danny, flashed into her mind, Danny whom she had petted and spoiled, whom she had turned into an ally in her fight with her parents - little, mischievous Danny, who had grown up and gone to Australia. Would he have gone - No! No! She mustn't think of that. The point was she had failed him as she had failed all of those who loved her. And now she was being given a chance to make amends.

"Ganesha," she addressed his statue, "you are the god that helps people to overcome obstacles. What should I do? Should I mind my own business or should I try to rescue this child?"

She noticed that Ganesha held an axe in his upper right hand and she took this as a sign that she should act, using force if necessary.

Once she had made up her mind, there were the practical steps to be considered. It would be useless going to Mr. Burke - from what she had heard of him, he wasn't the type to be swayed by a woman's pleas. In that case she would have to take direct action. Who knew how long the Pooka would survive in captivity? She had read of African slaves dying of heartbreak on the ships taking them to America. Couldn't the same thing happen to a wild boy held in a shed, especially one who had been used to roaming the open bog and mountain? The sooner she got to Lackendarragh the better. But first she would have to look for some tools.

Having searched the caravan without success, Maeve eventually found what she wanted in Jimmy Mac Dermott's carthouse. So it was that almost three hours after Aidan and Eithne had left her, she was tramping through the heather, a willow stick in one hand, a plastic bag containing sandwiches, a flask of tea, a rusty hacksaw and a screwdriver in the other. She followed the same route she had taken on the previous visit to Slieve Brack but instead of climbing the mountain, she continued around its lower slopes until, tired and perspiring, she came to a wood with mature oak trees. Blackbirds and chaffinches were singing among its yellowy-green leaves and speckled, brown butterflies danced in the sunlit glades.

After many false turns, she took a path that led to an open area dominated by the ruins of an imposing mansion. Following the beech-lined avenue on the other side for about half a mile, she found herself at the ornate entrance gate. There was a stone shed beside the gatehouse and after assuring herself that there was nobody within sight, she approached it.

Could this be the right place? There was a new padlock on the door bolt. Anxiously she listened then knocked. No sound came from within, not even an echo. In a low, urgent voice she called out, "Anybody here?" She repeated the question and thought she could hear a faint whimper.

Delaying no longer, she took out the screwdriver. While she was trying to loosen the screws she heard voices and retreated behind a beech tree. Two boys were climbing over the padlocked entrance gate, which was about nine feet high, with spikes at the top. With a sinking heart she recognised P.J. Durcan and Charlie Gallagher. It looked as if her rescue attempt would have to be abandoned.

The pair approached the shed. To judge from their loud curses, they were obviously not expecting to find it padlocked. A thought occurred to her: why not enlist them as accomplices? She could pretend that she only wanted to see the Pooka.

They were startled when she called out a breezy hello but accepted her explanation for coming.

"How did you find out about him being kept here?" P.J. asked suspiciously.

"I won't ask how you found out if you don't ask how I found out," Maeve smiled. "Anyway, I thought you boys were supposed to be in school?"

"We had a half day," Charlie explained. "A staff meeting; so we cycled out as soon as we got off the bus."

"I'll tell you what," Maeve proposed, "why don't you, P.J., keep a lookout by the gatehouse while Charlie and I go to work on the lock?"

"Why can't Gallo keep the lookout?" P.J. objected but Charlie told him that if he stood there nattering either Big Jim Burke or one of his men would be likely to surprise them.

Charlie had no more success with the screwdriver than Maeve had so they decided to use the hacksaw. The link of the padlock, however, proved too tough for the rusty blade.

"Why don't we cut off the lug holding the bolt?" Maeve suggested.

Charlie sawed furiously and when he tired, Maeve took over. While she was wondering if the attempt wasn't hopeless, P.J. came hurrying up.

"I think I can hear a truck back in the wood," he announced nervously.

"Okay," Maeve said. "You go up the avenue and keep a lookout there."

P.J. went off and she watched Charlie sawing at the lug.

"Hurry!" she pleaded. Next moment the blade snapped.

"Damn it!" she cried. "Why didn't I keep my big mouth shut?"

"Give me the screwdriver," Charlie remained calm. Inserting the screwdriver in the lug hole, he tried to bend the partially cut metal to one side. It gave a little. Encouraged, he put on more pressure. The screwdriver snapped.

"That's it!" Charlie said disgustedly.

"No, it's not," Maeve picked up a stone. At that moment P.J. came running up.

"There's a truck coming down the avenue!" he shouted and raced for the gate.

"Come on, Miss," Charlie tugged at her sleeve.

"No," Maeve cried. "You go. It's okay."

As Charlie followed P.J., she placed the shaft of the screwdriver in the hole and hit the top with the stone. The shaft fell out but she noticed that there was only a thin sliver of metal holding the lug. The thudding of the truck engine was now clearly audible. Using all her strength, she hit the lug repeatedly with the stone. It broke.

At first, the link of the padlock wouldn't pass through the gap in the lug but after some frantic twisting, she forced it out. Quickly she pulled back the bolt. The thudding of the engine grew louder.

CHAPTER 17

Gerg lay curled up in the fusty straw. Earlier that sunup, after Duach's departure, Crumale had brought more food and drink. Gerg had an almost uncontrollable urge to charge through the open door but Lacheen, armed with a heavy stick, stood in it. After they had left, he had succeeded in getting a handgrip on the top of the wall, only to find that the roof would not yield to the strongest push. Nevertheless, he had tried again and again, even thrusting at the iron sheets with his good foot while he clung to a rafter with both hands. Finally, he had dropped to the floor, too disheartened to continue.

He could hear the voices of his woodland friends like the music of a lost paradise: the soothing cooing of Kulure the Pigeon, the clear, sweet song of Lon the Blackbird, the metallic crow of Gleoite the Pheasant and, on one occasion, the exotic double note of Cuach the Cuckoo. They did not know of his predicament and even if they did, what could they do? Crumale had caught him, so he was doomed.

Minute after minute crawled by and still Gerg did not move. He watched Francach slinking up to the fresh food and nibbling it but he did not protest. A bee entered under the door, buzzed angrily about the nest-place, then blundered out again. Gerg sunk into a dream in which Suairc and the other hens returned from foraging and told him about their encounters with Nooma and the giant crutin; then they gathered round him, urging him to rise up and come out with them but no matter how hard he tried, he couldn't move.

Suddenly he jerked awake. Somebody was calling. Who was it? He held his breath while Francach scurried away through the straw. The call was repeated, low and urgent. It must be Nooma! Despite himself he whimpered a response. At once scratching sounds began outside the door, followed by crutin chattering, then more scratching sounds. This gave way to a metallic rasping that, with occasional pauses, went on and on until he thought his head would split. Later there were sharp clangs then a grating CRACK, succeeded by a dull CLANK, and light flooded into the nest-place. A dark shape filled the opening. If it was Nooma she would lock him in again. He must get out! Now!

Gathering his legs under him, he scampered on all fours past the advancing figure, ignoring the cry of alarm it emitted. Once outside, he rose to an upright position and sprinted as fast as his wounded foot would allow to the opposite trees. He heard more crutin cries behind him but he did not pause. A growling monster was thudding down the track between the beeches and Lacheen was racing through the field outside them. Going on all fours, he scrambled behind a briar patch and lay face down, so that he resembled a clump of withered grass. When Lacheen charged past, he took to his heels again and dodging from tree to tree, eventually reached the great stone nest-place and the wood beyond.

As the Pooka shot by her, Maeve staggered, crying out in fright. Recovering her balance, she rushed to the door in time to glimpse a half-naked boy disappearing through the trees on the far side of the avenue. The sound of the oncoming truck warned her that it was too risky to follow the Pooka. Forgetting her sandwiches, tools and willow stick, she fled up a path alongside the beeches. Warned by the deafening roar of the engine, she crouched behind a whitethorn bush. As she did so she glimpsed Johnno racing past the trees across from her. Presently a red trailer-truck heaved into view, smoke belching from its vertical exhaust pipe. Slowly but inexorably it advanced. As it growled and shuddered past, she could see that the trailer was carrying unsawn oak trunks, its hydraulic arm resting on the topmost one. In another minute it would reach the shed.

With a feeling of panic, she again began to run, though her wellingtons slowed her down. Keeping to the cover of the trees, she skirted the ruined mansion and making her way parallel to the path by which she had come, eventually arrived at the edge of the wood. Her breath came in hot sobs and her legs felt as if they would collapse under her. Some large animal bounded from a laurel thicket and she almost screamed with terror, before realising it was probably only a deer.

It wasn't until she had left Lackendarragh behind and was once more trudging through the heather at the foot of Slieve Brack that she began to relax. Why had she run away like a criminal? She should have stood her ground and faced any charges made against her. Wasn't it Mr. Burke who should be feeling guilty, not she? He had locked up the Pooka in that dirty, windowless shed and, on top of that, he was cutting down beautiful trees that must have taken a hundred years just to reach maturity - and, chances were, he would never replace them. But maybe she was being hasty: a good reporter should establish the facts.

As he sat with Johnno in the passenger seat of the trailer-truck Big Jim Burke reviewed his plans. They would halt at the gatehouse in order to cover the oak trunks with a tarpaulin sheet, which had been stored in the living room. After the load had been concealed, Noel, the driver, would continue on to Dublin for the ferry trip across to Holyhead. Mr. Hunt had phoned that morning with the address of a London furniture company that he had selected. If the company liked the quality of the timber - and that was a dead cert - big money would be offered and Mr. Hunt would see that his foreman got a suitable bonus. Between that and his success in capturing the Pooka he would be riding high.

Mr. Hunt had been somewhat vague about the Pooka, suggesting that his foreman should use his own discretion on how best to deal with the problem. He had taken the same tack the year before last when he had phoned him about dumping the cars and vans in the bog. Mr. Hunt preferred not to know about such problems: why was he paying a foreman good money if not to deal with them? Well, that being the case, Big Jim had followed his instincts. It didn't take him long on this occasion to decide that he would send the Pooka to England - Noel could leave him behind at a service area on the M-1 where he would be sure to be found. The English with their compassion for outcasts and dumb animals would treat him well and, without a doubt, he would be better off than he was in Lackendarragh.

Of course, there must be absolute secrecy about the entire venture. Even though Mr. Hunt had obtained an export licence for the oaks, if the Green freaks got wind of the operation they would be sure to kick up a stink. That was why Big Jim had decided to begin work in the heart of the wood, well out of sight of passers-by. By the time people got wise to what was going on it would be too late to stop the felling. As for the Pooka, he had in his pocket a sedative that would keep him quiet on the trip across - he had already put some in the sandwiches. If he was discovered under the tarpaulin by custom officials, Noel could pretend he was a stowaway.

Big Jim began to whistle, as he always did when feeling pleased, then he spied something darting across the avenue near the gatehouse.

"Did you see that?" he demanded.

"See what?" Johnno asked.

"It looked like a deer," Noel said.

"It looked like the Pooka," Big Jim corrected him. "Slow down! Johnno, run down that field just in case I'm right. Go on! Hurry up, man!"

When the trailer-truck picked up speed once more, Big Jim was no longer whistling.

95

CHAPTER 18

Once his fear of being overtaken passed, Gerg slowed to a trot. Soon he was deep among the great oaks and his heart sang. The delicate ferns, the new leaves, the mosses on the fissured barks glowed in the brilliant light, while speckled, brown butterflies fluttered here and there. To rest his wounded foot he crawled into a clump of laurels and hid. Dreoileen the Wren scolded him for intruding on his territory but when Gerg answered him in his own language, Dreoileen quietened down. Then the sound of clomping footsteps set him off again. Presently, Gerg saw a blue-clad crutin approaching rapidly.

"Nooma," he whispered, shivering with excitement. It must have been she who had opened the door! He crouched down, refusing to budge even when Dreoileen flew off. In a little while, Nooma, panting loudly, was alongside his hiding place. How brightly her cheek glowed, like a rowan berry or the first star after sundown! Then she was gone, moving noisily towards the edge of the wood. Should he try to follow? No, his foot was too sore. He would wait till the pain eased then he would somehow make his way to the hazel culleen, maybe on the back of Caoilte the Stag. From there he would be able to limp to the white nest-place.

It was evening when Maeve reached the caravan. A shower of rain had caught her in the open so that she was wet and shivering. She changed into dry clothes and treated herself to a hot meal of scrambled eggs, bread and beef tea. Afterwards, she took out her paints and paper and made a water colour of Lackendarragh, with the great oaks shouldering a blue sky and the Pooka, small and alone, gazing up at them. An idea occurred to her; she drew the red trailer-truck entering the green shade of the wood. It added, she decided, a really sinister touch.

Did Mr. Hunt know about the oaks being cut down? Of course he did. Hadn't Eileen McGreevy said that he owned the land from Eastersnow to Lackendarragh? And wasn't Big Jim Burke his foreman? There was something rotten in the state of Denmark ... But was she jumping to conclusions again? She would write to Michael and ask him to send down a photographer. If Mr. Hunt was about to fell one of Ireland's few remaining oak woods, they needed proof.

In the meantime, she would have to figure out some way of helping the Pooka before he harmed himself or somebody else. The saucers of milk she had put out at night following the return of the ankh hadn't been touched so far, though the reason for that was now clear.

Suppose he came back from Lackendarragh tonight - how would she convince him that she was a friend? Talk to him? No, he probably didn't understand human speech. And then the answer came to her: music!

She had heard of wild animals being soothed by music and once she had seen a television programme in which fish swam round and round a submerged loudspeaker playing waltzes. If only she had brought a radio with her ... But she had something - the recorder. It was a gift from her mother, who had been given it by her mother. She recalled the music lessons she had been sent to on Saturday mornings; the teacher had been quite impressed with her progress. Then she had got fed-up with the endless practising and despite her mother's pleas, had given it up. After her mother died, she had started practising again. Now, grateful that she had packed it with her painting materials, she took it out and began to play.

In the silence of the caravan the notes poured out, sweet and intoxicating. She tried different airs: folk songs, classical pieces and, finally, one of her childhood favourites:

> 'Here we go gathering nuts and may,
> Nuts and may, nuts and may;
> Here we go gathering nuts and may
> On a cold and frosty morning.'

Since today was May Day it seemed an appropriate tune to end with, though how one could gather nuts and may at the same time was beyond her. Her mother had once told her off for bringing may - as she called whitethorn blossoms - into the house. It would bring them bad luck. Maybe it had …

Her thoughts were interrupted by a loud knocking that caused her heart to miss a beat. Who could be visiting at this hour? She peeped through the lace curtain and saw a man of about thirty, casually dressed but respectable looking. When she opened the door, he put on an engaging smile and introduced himself as "Mossy Lalor, freelance journalist".

"And what do you want with me?" she asked, beguiled by his familiar Dublin accent.

"Can I sit down, Miss Duignan?" he evaded her question. "I left the car above at the road and my feet are killing me."

She decided that he could be trusted and allowed him to enter. His eye travelled round the cluttered interior before coming to rest on the water colour.

"So you're an artist too," he managed to convey both admiration and amazement in his comment.

"Why 'too'?" she offered him a chair, taking the other one herself.

"I heard you playing as I was crossing the bridge," he sat down gratefully, "and for a minute I thought I was listening to James Galway."

"Only for 'a minute'?" she smiled. "And what brings you to Eastersnow, Mr. Lalor?"

"Mossy," he protested. "I was informed by a contact of mine of your decision to come here to live and I thought it would make a good feature for *The Irish Times*."

"Oh, you're well established then," she bantered, "though I imagine the *Times*' readers would find my story rather boring."

"Far from it," he assured her. "What you're doing here ties in with the Green Movement, getting back to nature, all that …"

"You're interested in the Green Movement then?" she wondered if he had ever read any of Silvia's articles.

"Only as a journalist," he admitted. "Like yourself, I was brought up in the city. You must find this quite a change from Castleknock?"

"A change for the better," she remarked.

"Go on," he encouraged, taking out a pad and ball-point pen.

"Well, our world …," she hesitated. "It seems to be obsessed with material concerns, running after wealth and possessions, and all the time the spirit is being starved. People are dying of hunger in the Third World and there's real poverty in our own country - but that's because we're too selfish to share what we have."

"But you've left your job in GIVE," he pointed out. "How can living in a caravan in the heart of a bog help people in the Third World?"

"I know," she held out her hands, palms up. "But I have to get myself sorted out before I can help others. I'm trying to prove to myself how little of the goods in our consumer society we really need. Take, for example, wood. Do you know that the average person in the developed world uses 500 pounds of pulpwood each year and the average Third World resident uses 11 pounds?"

"Your point being?" he held his pen poised.

"That we're denuding this planet of trees to support our wasteful lifestyles," she spoke with passion. "We're cutting down beautiful trees that took years and years to grow so that we can have more paper tissues, cardboard boxes and disposable nappies."

"Is that why you painted the red truck in the forest?" he indicated the water colour.

"That's very perceptive of you," she was genuinely impressed.

"And who's the little fellow in the centre?" he went on. "The Pooka?"

"The what?" she pretended to be puzzled.

"The Pooka," he repeated.

"Surely you don't believe in such nonsense?" she knew now what he had really come about.

"I'm not so sure that a smashed JCB is nonsense," he regarded her shrewdly. "I've seen it myself at the garage."

"Listen, Mr. Lalor," she rose stiffly, "it's getting late and I'm very tired."

"All right, Maeve," he rose too. "But I would remind you that if you want to help this non-existing Pooka, you should tell me anything you know. Once the public have read my article, nobody will risk harming him."

"The power of the press," she scoffed. "And what sort of article will it be?" One of the DEVIL APPEARS IN COUNTY BALLROOM variety?"

"Yes, the power of the press," he ignored her question. "You and I, Maeve, know that without a vigilant press the men of wealth will bleed this country dry. Here's my card. I'm returning to Dublin tonight but I'll be back in Raheen this weekend. If you change your mind, give me a call."

CHAPTER 19

Two star-times passed before Gerg visited Eastersnow. His foot hurt more than ever but Caoilte - who had now lost his second horn - carried him to the culleen and he limped the rest of the way, crossing the river by the crutin bridge. Gealach's bright crescent was sinking below the horizon when he stopped by the white nest-place and began his song to Nooma, telling her of his loneliness, his reasons for running away when she opened the door, and the tasty roots he had brought her. Presently footsteps sounded inside then light flickered and glowed through the windows. Gerg crouched, ready to flee.

Roused from sleep by the Pooka's eerie singing, Maeve put on her dressing gown, lit a candle and picked up the recorder. When the singing stopped, she nervously put the wooden mouthpiece to her lips. If she played the tunes that Danny had liked as a boy perhaps the Pooka would like them too. Softly at first then with increasing power, she played "Ye Banks and Braes O' Bonnie Doon". No sooner had she finished than a short burst of crowing like the crowing of the grouse on Slieve Brack rang out. Encouraged, she launched into "Danny Boy" then switched to the lively "Phil the Fluter's Ball". Now the moment of truth had come ...

While Gerg crouched, a piping more bubbling than the liquid notes of Crotach the Curlew, more melodiously distinct than the lost cries of Maon the Golden Plover, more continuous and exquisite than the airy warbling of Donn the Skylark, came from the nest-cave, causing him to stand upright. He listened transfixed, shivers of excitement coursing up his spine, till the piping stopped. Then he crowed with excitement, Kok Kok Kok-Kok Kok Kok!

101

The piping began again, this time like the wavering, haunting lament of the breeze through sedges when the snow covers the mountains, and just as he thought his heart would break with loneliness, the piping changed into the laughter of water cascading down a mountain stream-bed when rain melts the snow; and he wanted to laugh too, to jump up and down, to tumble head over heels, to bound about like a lamb in the season of new buds.

Before the piping ended he laid the roots on the doorstep and backed away, so that when the door opened unexpectedly he was already beyond reach of the light. He saw Nooma pick up the roots. Then she placed a short reed in her mouth and the piping leaped out at him, taking away his strength, drawing him into the light despite his wish to be gone. He saw Nooma's eyes watching him above her quivering fingers, felt her power moving his tongue so that it was calling out, "Nooma! Nooma!" then he was standing before her, his eyes dazzled with the light, tears streaming down his cheeks.

With her heart in her mouth Maeve opened the door. She could detect two eyes shining faintly in the darkness. As she prepared to step further out, her bare foot struck against something and bending down, she discovered a few dirty roots like miniature parsnips. Judging that they were intended as a gift, she slipped the roots into the pocket of her dressing gown and began playing Brahms' Lullaby softly and caressingly. To her great joy she saw the eyes move towards her till she could distinguish the outline of a head and body and then a gaunt, grotesque little face that seemed too small for the great, luminous eyes, a face like that of one of the starving children of Sudan or Eritrea. Horrified she heard the child call out "Nooma! Nooma!", a thin bleating cry such as a lost lamb might make. In a daze she saw tears trickling from the child's eyes, then the pain and the horror overcame her and she screamed out, "No! No! No!", screamed against a world where such things could exist, screamed against the karma or fate that caused such things to happen, screamed against her own past mistakes that allowed suffering to flourish.

When she recovered her self-control, the child had disappeared and she was clinging to the door jamb. Sick at heart, she closed the door and sat down at the table with her head resting on her arms. Oh God, what had she done? Why had she spoiled everything with her hysterics? In her pride she had overestimated her own strength, her ability to accept this strange beast-child. No wonder Jimmy had fired his gun at him. She had thought herself more courageous than the old bachelor, had regarded him as the victim of an overactive imagination. How wrong she had been! Just as she had been wrong in the case of Danny ... thinking she knew better than her parents how to raise him ...

Half distracted, she took out the roots and laying them on the table, stared at them in horrified fascination. Was this his chief food? During the Great Famine, Irish people had eaten such things, as well as watercress and nettles. She would boil them tomorrow and taste them. Maybe they were more nutritious than potatoes or carrots, though she doubted it.

"Poor little Pooka," she murmured, "how can you survive on this fare?" An image of famine children, bones protruding through their skin, eyes resigned to death, flashed into her mind and she winced. Was man no more than this?

She got on her knees and begged God to guide her steps along the right path. As if in answer to her prayer, she saw herself talking to Jimmy about his last years in Eastersnow. If she could find out the truth about the Pooka's birth it would give her more insight into his predicament. It might also enable her to counteract the sensational report which she felt certain that hack, Lalor, was preparing. He would probably sell it to one of the English tabloids, which would have a field day depicting the Irish as superstitious peasants. Already she could visualise the headlines: "POOKA HAUNTS IRISH BOG" or "ARTIST CLAIMS TO HAVE MET POOKA".

Thank God, she had shown him the door before he had coaxed information out of her. And, yet, in one sense he might have been right: an honest journalist might just be the kind of champion the Pooka needed. Didn't it say in the Bible "The truth will set you free"? No doubt, Lalor would reply to that, "What is truth?" But she was judging people again, she who had made her parents' life a living hell and refused to see any point of view but her own.

Despite her will, an image rose in her mind, her mother smiling at Danny after he had won a prize for a school colouring competition. Why had her mother never smiled like that at her, even when she had won first prize in the RTE art competition? No, it was always Danny who was praised and made much of. Even her father would not take her side for fear of offending her mother. Poor Dad, always prepared to sacrifice her on the altar of domestic peace!

And then she saw her mother sending her up to bed for breaking a vase. She was calling out, "No, Ma! No, Ma!" but her mother just turned the key and locked her in. When she started to pound on the door, her father came and threatened to beat her if she didn't stay quiet.

Another image crowded in on her, the look on her mother's face when she had come home drunk from a disco. Was that the look the Pooka had seen on her face just now? Disbelief! Horror! Disgust!

"Oh God," she groaned, "I've made such a mess of things. Give me a chance to make amends. Help me find the Pooka before it's too late."

CHAPTER 20

When he observed the horror on Nooma's face and heard her cry out in that shrill voice, Gerg turned and scurried off. He had seen Foomnach the Vixen and Skatha the She Otter drive away their grown-up cubs with such displays of hostility, yet his heart burned with shame and anguish. Why had he fooled himself into thinking Nooma would want him? She had always kept him from her, always shut him in the hens' nest-place. If it hadn't been for the consolation of Suairc's clucking he would have died ages ago of loneliness. Now he knew there was no going back. He would seek out his friends, Tuan and Fand the Heather Fowl, whose presence would remind him of Suairceen, the little one that he had reared.

Despite the pain in his foot, he reached the culleen before sunup. In the first light that heralds the approach of Grian the stags were heading for an expanse of sweet grass that lay southeast of the culleen. This had once been a potato field but the Harte family that had worked it had all died during the Great Famine, leaving only their name. As Gerg came limping up, the stags paused to sniff the air, then continued on their way. Patiently he followed, knowing they would not go elsewhere till they had grazed. He passed the time searching for plantain leaves, some of which he ate, others he bound on his wounded foot with chords of twisted grass.

When Caoilte began grazing near him, he managed to climb onto his back. Waiting till the herd was facing the Great Hill, he suddenly emitted an alarm bark. Immediately the stags took to their heels. He clung to the rough hair of Caoilte's neck, grateful for his bounding suppleness but too heavy-hearted to enjoy it.

In no time the herd was entering the pine wood on the

Great Hill, where they slowed to a walk. Gerg slipped off Caoilte's back and made his way on all fours to the nest-cave he had once shared with Duach the Badger. Though the grass-grown entrance was barely wide enough to admit his body, inside it opened into a square tunnel with stone walls and a flat, stone roof. At one point where Duach's family had dug a side tunnel, the floor was covered with a pile of hardened clay. The stone tunnel continued beyond this obstruction and ended in a small chamber, too low to enable him to do more than crouch. Long ago when the ring fort was inhabited, grain and ale had been stored here and in times of attack, women and children had huddled fearfully in the stifling darkness.

Unaware of all this, Gerg wriggled into the chamber, which he had lined with plastic bags, heather and moss. In one corner there was a sack with two mangolds but he did not feel like eating. Lying on his side, he tried to sleep but though he felt exhausted, his mind kept tossing this way and that, as if he were still on Caoilte's back. For ages he twisted in the liquid dark, wishing Suairceen were with him. But Suairceen was gone and Nooma had turned into a stranger. There was nobody to comfort him now, for no matter how plentiful his friends, Nooma's return had awoken longings in him no gagna could satisfy. He was different from the stags, who were content to sleep and graze and in the time of leaf-fall, fight each other for mates; he was even different from the heather fowl, his closest companions, for while they could fly, he could not. Gathering himself into a tight ball, hands clasping his knees, he began to whimper softly.

Unconsciously, he must have drifted into sleep because when a sharp TIC-TIC-TIC roused him, the wall of the chamber showed up faintly in the gloom. Rolling over, he began to wriggle towards the irritating ticking. Dreoileen the Wren, who had been hunting for spiders in the tunnel entrance, flew away at his approach. The light hurt his eyes and the cheerful singing of birds pierced his ears like briar thorns. His mouth tasted bitter and he felt as if a great rick of peat sods had fallen on his head.

There was no use going on like this; now that his foot was wounded, things would only get worse. He would climb to the top of a pine tree and throw himself down. After that, his shadow would fly to the island in the Bright Lake, where Gealach rested during suntime. Once there, he would meet Suairc and Suairceen and be lonely no more.

Without bothering about Crumale and his crutins, he wandered about openly in search of a suitable tree. At last he came to one at the edge of the wood and climbed it, ignoring the scolding of Skradogue the Jay, who had a nest in a nearby whitethorn.

Picking a high branch that bent under his weight, he gazed through the pale green needles at the remains of a wall. If he launched himself far enough outward, he would crash onto the mossy stones. A vision of his mangled, blood-drenched body flashed into his mind, and he closed his eyes to regain his courage. Slowly he opened them, drew a deep breath and trembling in every limb, crouched.

Kok Kok Kok-Kok! At that precise moment Tuan's alarm crow rang out. Squinting at the greenish-brown slope in front of him, Gerg saw through a haze of pain Nooma ascending the Great Hill. Hope came flooding into his mind so that he reeled and clutched wildly at a branch to stop himself from falling.

He watched Nooma's blue-clad figure slowly moving higher and higher. She must have disturbed Tuan when she was passing through his territory. What was she up to? Did she expect to find him in his nest-cave in the cairn?

Iorra the Red Squirrel came scampering up the tree but Gerg did not turn his head. He was waiting till Nooma would disappear over the brow of the Great Hill. As soon as she did, he began to climb down from his branch, ignoring the pain when the sole of his injured foot gripped the bark. At last he

reached the ground and crawling under the wire fence, he slid feet first into the drain, scaled the far bank and crept into the heather.

Afraid that Nooma might spot him if he climbed to the top, he decided to await her return. While lying in a peat hag, or bare patch, he heard a faint cheeping. Raising his head, he emitted a series of low chuckles and, presently, Fand, accompanied by tiny balls of mottled down, emerged from cover. Gerg's heart sang. What lovely chicks they were, just like Suairceen when he rescued her! They scurried round him, busily searching for insects. He found them moths and spiders, which they nibbled, their little beaks tickling his fingers.

By and by there was the sound of distant footsteps and Fand and the chicks melted into the surrounding vegetation. Peeping out through a screen of heather, Gerg saw Nooma descending. For what seemed an eternity he remained motionless until her blue form had disappeared among the pine trees. Then leaving the peat hag, he began to weave his way up to the crest.

Soon he was mounting the cairn and approaching his nest-cave. At the entrance he paused, intoxicated by the aroma of crutin and food. Every sense alert, he edged into the interior.

The first thing that met his eye was his old, blue-figured eating bowl with bread and some other food in it, the whole covered with soft, shiny stuff that looked like a dragonfly's wing. Beside the bowl, Nooma's looped object, now attached to a tendril of metal, rested on a square, brightly coloured leaf. Why had she brought it back? Was it because of the roots he had given her?

And his eating bowl! Were the tiny crutins still crossing the bridge and the two birds still meeting in mid-air above them? Oh, how happy he felt now and only a short time ago he had been on the point of jumping off the tree!

Eagerly he picked up the looped object and let it rest in the palm of his hand, surrounded by its tendril. What would he do with it? Should he take it back to Nooma with the empty bowl or did she expect him to keep it. Then his eye fell once more on the square, brightly coloured leaf. Carefully he turned it around with the toes of his injured foot. To his amazement he saw figured on it, as clearly as in a still pool, himself standing in front of Nooma, whose hands rested on his shoulders. The looped object was hanging from his neck by the metal tendril and both he and Nooma were smiling.

CHAPTER 21

Hunched in the passenger seat of the Volkswagen beside Mr. O'Connor, Maeve squeezed her fingers tightly. What if she were the fool rushing in where angels fear to tread? Jimmy Mac Dermott might have nothing worthwhile to tell her - and what if her suspicions were ill-founded? She would have liked to discuss the matter with Mr. O'Connor but he looked tired after his day's work in the shop and Sunday was supposed to be a day of rest. No doubt he must have thought she had some neck to ask for a lift to the Nursing Home at this hour? And though she had got what she wanted, she felt as she had felt that summer in London before news of her father's death reached her, that things were heading towards some nameless disaster. Too many things were happening too quickly and she was exhausted.

She reviewed the morning's activities: getting up at first light to pray and then as if in answer to her plea for guidance, some inner voice telling her that she should use her talent as an artist to communicate with the Pooka. She had immediately painted a water colour of herself and the boy in the mother-and-son pose she had often adopted with Danny while they stood in front of the wardrobe mirror. In a flash of inspiration she had shown the ankh hanging from his neck, knowing that if she could get him to wear it, people would realise he wasn't some sort of wild animal. Wasn't that why her mother had always made sure that Tom, their cat, wore a collar?

Next, her eye had fallen on Ganesha and she had been struck by the fact that in his lower left hand he held a string of beads and in his lower right a bowl of sweets. That was it! If her ankh was the equivalent of the beads, then what would be the equivalent of the sweets? She remembered the roots the

Pooka had brought her. Would he eat shop food? Hoping he would, she had placed bread and cheese in the willow-pattern bowl and covered food and bowl with cling film. She noticed as she did so that Ganesha carried a broken tusk in his upper left hand. Would that be the equivalent of the broken screwdriver?

When she had got home from her trip to Slieve Brack and was looking forward to a chance to recover, who had arrived but Charlie Gallagher and the O'Connor children. In a way, it had been a godsend. Once she had told them of the glimpse she had obtained of the fleeing Pooka, she had sworn them to secrecy. If the news reached the likes of Mossy Lalor, the story would be plastered across the front page of every newspaper.

While discussing her most recent water colours, she had learned that Charlie was an amateur photographer. She had immediately suggested that he take photos of the tree felling sites in Lackendarragh and the dump by the boreen. In addition, they should all try to find out what Big Jim Burke had been planning to do with the Pooka. That he suspected her of being involved in the Pooka's escape was clear from another piece of news: Mr. Hunt was no longer going to pay for her groceries.

Maeve had asked Aidan and Eithne if their father could drive her to Fennor, and when he had arrived after work, she had already written a letter to Michael requesting the low-down on Mr. Hunt. If he wanted to get tough then he would find she was no push-over. Mr. O'Connor had agreed to give her groceries on credit until she sold a few of her paintings. If this trip to Jimmy Mac Dermott confirmed her theory, then she was ready to do battle for the Pooka.

Her theory was that the Pooka was the child of Noreen Sweeney, who had been a happy girl till some calamity changed her. What greater calamity for a fourteen or fifteen-year-old than to become pregnant? Given the puritan code of country people, she would have seen herself as a fallen woman, a slut. Then the trauma of giving birth all alone in a field or byre would have robbed her of the power of speech. Maybe she had concealed her child in the henhouse, bringing him food in the willow-pattern bowl. That would explain why he had not died in the fire that had killed his mother and great-grandfather. It was the only logical explanation for his sudden appearance at that time.

But now his life could well be in danger. There was no guarantee that he would find the gifts she had left in the cairn, so that her hasty journey to Slieve Brack might have been a waste of time and effort. If Jim Burke came upon him before she did, anything might happen. Locking a half-wild boy like that up in a windowless shed might unbalance him mentally, especially if he had been locked up as a child. She recalled her own anger at her parents for curtailing her freedom, an anger that had finally led, after one fierce and violent argument, to her running away to London.

It was during her fourth year in London that her father died and her mother entered the Nursing Home. Her father had been buried by the time she learned the news from a Dublin friend she had run into one evening in a West End bar. Immediately, she booked a flight to Dublin but her trip home had been a disaster, with her mother staring at her with accusing eyes. As a result, she hurried back to London, where she tried to blot out reality in a drug-induced haze. It was at this time her mother entered the Nursing Home. The move was as unexpected as it was unnecessary. Her mother had plenty of relations who would have looked after her but she preferred to punish her daughter by acting the abandoned parent.

"Poor Mamma! How I must have hurt you to drive you to that extreme?" she thought. "If you had only let me make amends ... I know that I was a rebellious child but even the Prodigal Son was welcomed back ... If Dad had been alive, everything might have turned out differently ... I know he loved me - and that you loved me too - but I was too pig-headed at the time to see it ... And then Dad's heart attack - it wasn't my fault, was it, Mamma? He was always complaining of a pain in his left arm - you know he was ... Maybe my running away brought one on but it could have happened anyway - not that I'm defending my actions. If I can help this poor, lost boy, perhaps it will make up for some of the unhappiness I've caused ... He reminds me so much of Danny ..."

The nurse that met her at the entrance was at first reluctant to admit her because of the lateness of the hour but when she explained that the matter was urgent, she brought her to a waiting room. Jimmy eventually came, delighted with the break in routine. Soon he was puffing away at his pipe while she worked the conversation round to Noreen Sweeney.

"Well, now that you mention it," he mused, "she could have got pregnant. Do you know, I often thought the same myself - but sure who could have fathered the child and she living isolated over there?"

"Weren't there turf cutters during the summer?" she realised that the discussion was straying into a delicate area, yet for the sake of the Pooka she was determined to persist.

"There were," Jimmy puffed meditatively at his pipe. "We always got a dozen or so from the village - I even sold them turf banks myself. Still, they were decent people and even if one of them took advantage of the girl, there's the matter of time."

"How do you mean?" Maeve was genuinely puzzled.

"Well, it was summertime when she changed because I can remember that I was footing turf and the heather was in bloom," Jimmy pressed down the tobacco she had brought him with a crooked brown finger. "I called out to her as she was driving the goat home and where once she would have stopped for a laugh and a bit of conviviality, she just hung her head and hurried away. I mentioned it to her grandfather later but I saw he was reluctant to discuss it, so I kept my peace."

"But why should the fact that it was summertime rule out one of the turf cutters as the father?" Maeve persisted.

"Well ..., it's the nine months thing, you see," Jimmy was growing embarrassed. "I reckon it must have been autumn when she got pregnant, if the child was due in the summer."

"And who would have been around in the autumn?" Maeve asked.

"Fowlers," Jimmy removed his pipe and spat into the fireplace. "The grouse season opens in September and, as well as the local gunmen, there was always a few down from Dublin. Tom Hunt never missed a season."

"Mr. Hunt?" Maeve tried to keep her voice even.

"Oh, he was a great shot," Jimmy continued, "a real dinger. I've seen him down a brace of grouse with the left and right barrel at sixty yards. Oh, he was a fine man in those days, handsome and athletic. You'd walk many a long mile before you'd meet his equal. It's no wonder every girl in the village was out to catch him."

"And, of course, none of them did," Maeve recalled Eileen McGreevy saying that Mr. Hunt's wife was confined to a wheelchair as a result of a hunting accident and that he was very good to her.

"Not a chance of it," Jimmy smiled. "He married an English heiress, though I'm told they have no children. Still, I'm sure he's happy - and if he's not, it's not for the want of money."

"Marry for money, take a mistress for love," Maeve spoke her thoughts aloud.

"Well, being a bachelor, I wouldn't know about that," Jimmy's eyes twinkled. "But Tom Hunt was married a few years before the change came on Noreen."

"Do you know that he plans to buy up all the land north of Eastersnow River and turn it into a spruce plantation?" Maeve assumed that the trees would be Sitka Spruces.

"Well, the devil an inch of my land he'll ever plant," Jimmy spat into the grate, "for I'm told those damn spruces destroy the soil and the rivers. I'd rather see yourself, Maeve, living there than think of the place as one solid mass of evergreens."

"But I have no money to pay for your farm," Maeve pointed out.

"Money is it?" Jimmy removed his pipe from his mouth. "Sure what would an old codger like me want with money? I'd be happier thinking of yourself living in the old place than I'd be if I won a million in the Lotto."

CHAPTER 22

As he sat in O'Connor's pub with a pint of stout on the table before him, Big Jim Burke was far from happy. The immediate cause of his distress was Mossy Lalor, who was sitting opposite him, talking to a group of farmers. Big Jim could hear snatches of the conversation: "right to do what he likes ... ... own property ... ... employment ... ... all right for the gentry ... ... plant young oaks ..." It didn't take much savvy to conclude that they were discussing the felling at Lackendarragh. Just as he had feared, news of the Pooka had leaked out and now this smart alecky reporter from Dublin was getting his nose into matters that were none of his damn business. He would have to be neutralised.

The other thing that preyed on his mind was the phone call he had just had with Mr. Hunt. While he had clinched the deal with the furniture factory, Mr. Hunt thought it best to halt felling till the Pooka business cleared over. That meant the chain saws could be idle for months and his bonuses and overtime would be postponed. Mr. Hunt was coming down in person on Friday to assess things for himself. He obviously distrusted his foreman's ability to deal with the situation. Very well, he would show him. If the oak felling was halted then he would get the Sitka Spruce planting restarted.

The first thing to do was to clear the heather off the lower slopes of Slieve Brack; then the crawler tractors and ploughs could move in. There was one obstacle, however: the police might not give permission for heather burning this late in the year. They would have to make it appear that the fire was started maliciously. That would present no difficulties: it would be easy enough to lay the blame on young vandals from the village. If his own crew put on a show of fighting the fire when it was already well advanced, who would suspect them? Tomorrow was a bank holiday. They could start the fire while people were taking a lie-in or getting themselves ready for the races in Fennor.

Big Jim downed the remainder of his pint and with a gruff "Good evening, men" to the farmers, strode from the pub.

While Big Jim was walking home from O'Connor's pub and Maeve was returning from the Nursing Home, Gerg was limping back from the white nest-place. The western sky was still streaked with crimson but chill shadows stretched across the bog. He fingered the looped metal on his breast as if it were a living thing that could remove the pain from his foot. He spoke to it about Tuan and Fand and their new-born chicks, about Glic and Dreoileen and Caoilte, telling it that they were in need of protection from Crumale, who was filled with hatred for all gagna. Then he questioned it about Nooma. Why was she not in the white nest-place? Would she know that it was he, Gerg, who had left the root-filled eating bowl on the step? Would she come looking for him in the cairn at sun-up?

"Mah-ah-ah-ah-ah!" Naoscach the Snipe cried out from the inky blue vault above him like a kid goat bleating for its mother. He stopped to listen, his own loneliness stirred by the mournful, repeated cadence till he thought his heart would break. What if Nooma were only luring him back so that she could lock him up again? And yet she had brought him food as she used to do long ago and she had given him this looped metal, which was like no other object he had ever seen, and the small bright reflection of the two of them together. Nooma was a crutin and yet he was more like her than he was like Tuan and Fand. And Nooma had piped on her reed in a way that affected him as no gagna singing - not even Naoscach's - ever had. There was some power that was taking possession of him, drawing him out of the gagna world. Why else should he in full suntime and with one foot almost useless have ventured from the safety of the Great Hill to Nooma's nest-place? If Crumale and his crutins had sighted him, he would have been finished.

117

This thought was enough to goad him into moving on. Gritting his teeth, he struggled through moss and heather, sedge and sheugh, till he came to the firmer ground at the base of the mountain. Once among the trees his strength gave out, so that instead of climbing to the summit he crawled into his nest-cave under the ring fort and fell into an exhausted sleep.

The fumes from burning vegetation roused him. In a panic he scrambled into the sunlit open, where an intermittent, low crackling told him that the heather beyond the trees was on fire. Immediately he thought of Fand and her babies. Picking up a stick on which to lean, he hobbled as fast as he could to the edge of the wood.

The sight that met his eyes filled him with the same horrified fascination he had felt on seeing Nooma and the giant's nest-place burning. Driven by a stiff breeze, a wall of flame was eating its way uphill. Soon it would reach the level at which he waited, though since there was a stretch without heather outside the drain bordering the trees, he was in no danger. The same would not be true for Fand's babies, who would be stumbling frantically on their tiny legs to escape the smoke and heat.

As if in confirmation of this fear, Tuan rose crowing from the middle of the smoke and went whirring off to the far side of the mountain. A few moments later, Giorria came racing headlong towards the wood, leapt the drain in one reckless bound and threw himself repeatedly against the fence until he found a hole under the wire. Then, eyes bulging, he darted away.

Gerg watched Giorria disappearing down a woodland path. He did not blame him for his panic. All gagna feared the red, flickering tongues that devoured everything in their path. Those who could fled. It was only mother gagna, such as Fand, who stayed to do battle for their young.

An image of Fand half crazed with terror as the flames bore down on her cheeping babies flashed into Gerg's mind. He would not leave her to her fate as he had once left Suairc. But only a frog in water could survive such a conflagration -

a frog! Water!

Rushing back to the tunnel, he emptied the mangolds from the sack and taking it to the drain, doused it. Then he slung the dripping sack over his head and shoulders and clambered up the bank. Without further hesitation, he hobbled out into the blinding acrid smoke.

"Gobak! Gobak!" he crowed repeatedly as, eyes streaming, he plunged deeper and deeper into the inferno. Then he gave the chuckling crow with which the heather cock calls his mate but all he could hear in reply was the growling of the advancing monster. The smoke billowed into his face, choking him if he drew breath, then it would swirl away for an instant and he would gulp down air. The stick got lodged in wet peat so often that he finally threw it away and crawled forward on his hands and knees.

Now that he was nearer to the ground more of the smoke flowed and writhed above him but sometimes a shift in the breeze bore it all downward so that he coughed and spluttered, close to suffocation. Moss, heather, cotton-grass passed trembling before his eyes and blood pounded in his ears. He sank on his belly and slithered forward till he could glimpse fiery red tongues curling and flicking among the heather clumps. The heat was almost unbearable.

Somewhere behind him he heard crutin voices but he did not stop. With a kind of detached clarity he knew that he was trapped: if he continued going forward he would be burned alive and if he turned back the crutins would catch him. Groping under his sack, he touched Nooma's looped metal. Its hardness seemed to restore his strength. Emitting, over and over, an urgent, gasping chuckle, he headed into the flames.

Just as he felt that his lungs were ablaze, a disturbed clucking reached his ears. "Kok Kok Kok-kok Kok!" he crowed hoarsely, changing direction.

CHAPTER 23

On the east shoulder of Slieve Brack, not far from Lackendarragh Wood, Big Jim Burke and his men were filling knapsack sprayers from a small stream that over the centuries had cut an irregular channel down the mountain. They paused to watch the dense curtain of smoke with its crimson hem moving steadily towards them. As soon as it got within a hundred yards they would douse a swath of heather in its path then move in with dung forks to beat down the flames. A second dousing would quench most of the fire but if that didn't work, they could prevent it crossing the stream and it would eventually burn itself out.

"Hurry up there!" Big Jim bellowed. "You'd think you were at a funeral." Secretly he was pleased with the way things were going. The breeze was blowing in the right direction and the warm sunshine meant that the heather and sedge were dry. With a bit of luck they would be finished in plenty of time for a leisurely wash and a meal before driving to the races in Fennor. If it weren't for the possibility of one of the men letting slip how the fire had been started, he would be jubilant.

"Look!" Johnno's voice interrupted his thoughts. His eyes followed his helper's pointing finger.

"Bloody hell!" he stared in disbelief. "What's this?" A small brown figure was crawling downhill into the smoke.

"It's the Pooka!" Johnno gasped.

"I know it's the Pooka!" Big Jim snarled, "but what in hell is he up to? If I ever lay hands on the blackguard that let him out - Stay here, men!" he added, striding off.

Johnno followed him. By the time they reached the spot where they had last glimpsed the Pooka, the heat was so intense that they were unable to proceed.

"It's no use," Johnno said. "He'll never come out of that alive."

"The bloody fool!" Big Jim swore. "What in hell got into him?" He covered his nose with his handkerchief and made a last attempt to go forward but the flames drove him back.

"Come on!" he shouted. "We'll have to pretend we never saw him. Maybe it was only a fox, after all ..."

Two hours later, Maeve accompanied by Eithne and Aidan arrived at the smouldering, black slope. The children had been cycling down to the caravan with groceries when a great white cloud joining Slieve Brack to the sky caught their attention. Maeve confirmed that it was a cloud of smoke and deciding that there was no time to be lost, set out at once with the children for the mountain. Now with fear gripping her heart, she led the way among the charred heather twigs up towards the summit.

As she half expected, the nest in the cairn was empty. Her water colour of the Pooka and herself rested against a stone, where it could be easily viewed by someone lying or sitting down. Apart from that and the potato sack, there was no human artifact in the place. Did that mean that the Pooka was now wearing her ankh? She fervently hoped that it did.

Eithne and Aidan were amazed at the nest and her representation of the Pooka.

"He looks like one of those African children on T.V.," Eithne remarked, "except that he has long hair and a tunic. Was he really as dark as that?"

"I'm not sure," Maeve admitted. "Remember it was night-time when I saw him; and he is probably sunburnt as well."

Aidan lay down in the nest and decided it was too hard and cramped for his liking.

"If I spent a night in that, I don't think I'd get much sleep," he commented.

"That's because you're so soft," Eithne told him. "Now get up before your ruin it."

Leaving the willow-pattern dish filled with food as a gift,

they set off downhill, keeping close to the drain. Suddenly Eithne, who was in the lead, gave a scream. Further down, outside the broken wall bordering the drain, there was a barely noticeable heap that had two naked human legs protruding from it.

Controlling her panic, Maeve forced herself to go on but by the time she reached the limp form, Aidan was already kneeling beside it. The Pooka's hair was singed and grey with ashes and his sack-tunic was partly burned. There was another sack lying nearby. When Maeve searched for a pulse in his wrist and neck, she couldn't find any but her fingers encountered the chain of the ankh.

"Quick!" she commanded Aidan. "Fetch some water from the drain."

"But how will I carry it?" he asked.

"Here, take this," she removed one of her wellingtons and thrust it into his hand. "Now, Eithne, you'll have to be brave," she turned to the girl, who seemed on the point of fainting. "Help me to turn him over."

Eithne did as she was told, keeping her eyes averted. Maeve scrutinised the blistered, soot-stained face. The large eyes were closed, the mouth open, revealing even, yellow teeth and where the singed, matted locks fell back, the forehead was broad and unexpectedly pale. There was no sign of life. Nevertheless, she poured water from her wellington onto the singed hair and wetting her handkerchief, laid it gently on the closed eyes. There was no response.

"What will we do now?" Eithne asked.

"We'll have to carry him back to the caravan," Maeve was surprised at her own calmness; it was as if she were standing outside her own body, watching herself act. She knew now that Danny had never gone to Australia, that he had died after crashing the motorbike she had sent him money to buy. A week later her father had his heart attack. Was this how Danny would have looked, a heap of discarded flesh?

"We'll have to make a stretcher," she forced her mind back to the present. "Aidan, will you get two straight branches about six feet long. And, Eithne, help me tidy him up."

Using handfuls of moss, they proceeded to brush away dirt and ashes from the limbs, discovering in the process the burnt flesh beneath.

"Look at this foot!" Maeve exclaimed. "It's all swollen. And no wonder; there's an infected cut on the sole. I wouldn't be surprised if the poor child died of blood poisoning."

"Are you certain he's dead?" Eithne's voice quivered. "Isn't a corpse supposed to feel cold?"

"Yes," Maeve paused. "But then the day is so warm - and he may just have died."

Aidan returned with two half-rotten branches. "They were all I could find," he said.

"In that case," Maeve rose, brushing the hair back from her perspiring forehead, "we'll just have to go for help." She knew that she would become hysterical if left alone with the body and she couldn't very well ask the children to stay.

When they arrived back later in the afternoon with the doctor and three men from the village, there was no sign of the Pooka.

"He was lying just there," Maeve insisted. "You can see where the grass is flattened - and there's the moss we used to clean him! It's almost as if the ground opened and swallowed him up."

CHAPTER 24

The first thing that Gerg became aware of was the pain in his head. He opened his eyes but found he couldn't see. A grey fog enclosed him, except for lower down, where there was light near his nose. He raised his hand to brush the fog away. His fingers encountered a piece of damp sack, that he removed. Immediately, sunlight dazzled him. With infinite care he turned onto his side, while the outside world came reeling back. Was the red-tongued monster still devouring the heather? Fighting nausea, he raised his head. Beyond the green of grass and sedge, there were only charred twigs and ashes.

He closed his eyes, remembering how he had carried Fand and her chicks in the mangold sack. Just when he thought he couldn't endure the heat a moment longer he struck a swampy patch, where he crouched while the flames growled and crackled past. Then he was blundering through a smouldering wasteland, the hot ashes scorching his soles. At times he fell but he rose again and staggered on. When he reached the line of stones everything went blank.

Now he noticed the piece of white sack that had covered his eyes. There were blue and pink flowers in one corner and green leaves round the edge. On raising it to his nose he detected, beneath the odour of drain water, a lingering fragrance. It must be Nooma's! If she had put it on his eyes she must have touched his face. He felt a surge of joy: Nooma had found him but she hadn't locked him up. She had left this white sack-piece to entice him to her as a heather hen entices her chick with a white moth.

But he couldn't go to her - not yet. His whole body felt weak and his throat was parched. Somehow he must get to water. Turning, he crawled over the uneven line of stones and

slithered down into the drain. Kneeling, he drank from his cupped hands then buried his throbbing forehead in the cool trickle till the pain eased. Suddenly a thought struck him: he hadn't let Fand out of the sack!

When he reached the mangold sack it was empty. That meant that Fand and the chicks must have got out by themselves. Draping the sack over his shoulders, he slowly crossed the drain and crawled back to his nest-cave in the tunnel, the white sack-piece dangling from his teeth.

On Wednesday when Maeve opened the caravan door, she found the Pooka lying in a heap by the bottom step. A quick check told her that he wasn't dead. Overjoyed, she lifted him in her arms and carried him inside. He was surprisingly light and his sack-tunic didn't smell as badly as she expected. When she laid him on the floor he began to moan feebly. Her chain was still about his neck and when she pulled it up she found her handkerchief knotted beside the ankh.

How should she go about reviving him? She had done a first-aid course during the time she was hoping that Eileen would send her to Africa. Here was her chance to prove that she could have dealt with any emergency. Taking a basin of water and a cloth she washed the boy's face lightly. Then she washed his sore foot. If it was to have any chance of healing she would have to bathe it in warm water and disinfectant.

While the kettle was boiling she cradled the boy's head on her arm and spooned water between his partly open lips; most ran down his chin but she hoped he had swallowed the rest. After bathing his foot, she dipped her tweezers in the disinfectant and probed the wound. He did not react. To her amazement, she found a tiny splinter of glass embedded near the bone. When she removed it, the wound began to bleed. That was good. The blood would wash out impurities.

Bathing the wound once more, she covered it with ointment and put on a plaster bandage. An idea occurred to her: she slipped a plastic bag over the foot and tied it lightly at the ankle. By this time the boy's eyelids were flickering. She made a drink of beef tea and again cradling his head on her arm, spooned some into his mouth. Immediately he began to splutter. Recalling Jimmy Mac Dermott's practice, she tried him with milk and to her delight, he began to swallow spoonful after spoonful. As he did so she felt that he was conscious of her presence, though his eyes remained closed.

She began to croon Brahms' Lullaby and suddenly his eyes opened wide and he looked at her with the glazed look of a sick child. His irises were bluish-grey, flecked with hazel. It was an extraordinary experience watching those great eyes gazing at her out of the thin shrivelled face; they told of the spirit burning inside, the kinship between herself and this half-wild creature.

When he wouldn't drink any more, she placed the pillow gently under his head and covered him with a blanket. She would have to go for Dr. Farrell in case he needed penicillin. His eyes were again closed - but what if he came to while she was gone? He might go berserk on finding himself alone in an alien environment. Suppose he injured himself with a knife or accidentally turned on the gas? She couldn't tie him up and she couldn't lock him in.

Putting on her wellingtons and jacket, she carried the sleeping boy to Jimmy Mac Dermott's byre and placed him on the pile of hay under the loft. Then she returned with a bottle of water and a bag of sandwiches, which she left nearby. His eyes were still closed and he was breathing evenly. Tucking the blanket in around his frail body, she told him not to be anxious, that she would only be gone a little while. She hoped that the sound of her voice would somehow penetrate his mind and reassure him. Then she pulled the door of the byre to, but without closing it, and hurried away.

About half an hour after Maeve left Eastersnow Big Jim Burke and Johnno approached the caravan.

"Let's see what she has in here," Big Jim opened the door with a key.

"What are we supposed to be looking for, anyway?" Johnno stared in amazement at the water colours fixed to the wall and strewn on the table.

"Anything that can help us to nail her" Big Jim checked the toilet cubicle. "Drugs, letters, photos, that sort of thing."

"Photos of what?" Johnno's eye fell on the statue of Ganesha.

"Of the oak trees or the Pooka," Big Jim was rifling through Maeve's suitcase. "Mr. Hunt doesn't want any surprises when he talks to her on Friday. He had enough trouble with that reporter fellow, Lalor."

"But the Pooka died after the fire," Johnno began searching the bedside locker.

"Then why didn't Dr. Farrell and the others find his body?" Big Jim unzipped a pocket of the knapsack. "And what about that blanket in the byre above and the bottle of water?"

"It could have been some fellow that was sleeping rough," Johnno was examining a water colour of Slieve Brack.

"Will you put that damn picture down and search the cupboard?" Big Jim snapped. "We don't want her arriving back from Raheen before we're through - and while you're at it, take that elephant thing out of your pocket. I want everything left just as we found it."

CHAPTER 25

"Now, Miss Duignan, you don't really expect me to swallow all this nonsense about a Pooka?" Mr. Hunt sat across the caravan table from Maeve, his silver hair brushed neatly back, his pink complexion glowing with health.

"Ask your foreman, Mr. Burke, if you don't believe me," she kept her voice even, knowing this handsome, urbane businessman could quickly dismiss her as a hysterical woman, as Dr. Farrell had seemed to do.

"I have asked him," he tapped his manicured fingers gently together. "He told me it was just some village boys playing pranks."

"Then ask Aidan and Eithne O'Connor," Maeve met his sceptical gaze. "They were with me when I found the body." It was just as well, she decided, to keep quiet about the Pooka's later visit to the caravan and his disappearance from the byre. Dr. Farrell had practically accused her of making the whole thing up.

"Ah, O'Connor," Mr. Hunt smiled. "I seem to recall that that was one of the boys Mr. Burke suspected. You'll have to admit, Miss Duignan, that your story is a little ... well, shall we say, imaginative - especially as the body you speak of seems to have disappeared."

"About as imaginative as the story of a girl living in a bog who one day meets a handsome stranger and falls in love with him," she was delighted to see the smile fade from his face.

"I haven't the faintest idea what you're talking about," Mr. Hunt protested.

"I'm talking about Noreen Sweeney," she saw his face blanch. "I'm talking about the handsome stranger to whom, in her innocence, she gave herself. I'm talking about the son that was born to her and that, in her shame, she hid in a henhouse. I'm talking about that son escaping at the time Joe Sweeney and his granddaughter burned to death."

"You're saying Noreen Sweeney had a son?" there was the same hunted look in his eyes that she had once seen in her father's when she had accused him of going behind her back to complain about her to the school principal.

"Yes, I'm saying she had a son," she spoke with quiet conviction.

"And what proof do you have for the existence of this son?", Mr. Hunt's expression was a mixture of wariness and anguished hope.

"No proof other than circumstantial evidence and my instincts as a woman," she admitted. "I believe that Noreen Sweeney went dumb as a result of giving birth out there on her own, with nobody to turn to for help or understanding."

"So that's all it is?" his eyes became guarded. "Mere speculation?"

"No, it's not mere speculation," she knew she had lost ground. "I saw the Pooka, remember."

"Miss Duignan, living out here on your own has obviously affected your judgment," he was beginning to show a hint of the steel fist in the velvet glove. "If you really believe I'm the father of this imaginary creature you call the Pooka then you have either been hoodwinked by some local busybody or you are indulging in some absurd fantasy of your own."

"I'm not trying to prove a case in a court of law," Maeve tried another tack. "I'm trying to appeal to your conscience, Mr. Hunt. If you can look me in the eye and tell me that you never put Noreen Sweeney at risk of having a child, then I will withdraw my allegation." She saw him hesitate, saw him lick his dry lips. "Come, Mr. Hunt," she pressed home her advantage. "I have no intention of betraying your confidence. I'm trying to open your eyes to the truth."

"The truth?" he gave her a curious look. "What do you want of me?"

"I want you to turn all the property you own in this area - Eastersnow, Slieve Brack, Lackendarragh - into a nature reserve," she spoke quietly. "It could be called '*Pairc a' Phúca*, The Pooka's Park', or 'The Hunt Nature Reserve'."

"WHAT?" he gasped. "You must think me a fool, Miss Duignan? It was I who gave you the use of this caravan, free, gratis and for nothing, and it was I who paid for your food till you decided to interfere in my affairs."

"You mean by freeing the non-existing Pooka?" she met his gaze fearlessly. "I'm grateful for your help, Mr. Hunt, but I won't let it blind me to what you're engaged in here. I've seen what your men are doing in Lackendarragh - cutting down the oaks. I know of your plan to cover this entire area with evergreens."

"And is it now a crime for a man to develop his own property as he sees fit?"

"Yes, your sort of development is a crime, a crime against nature."

"And didn't God create nature for our benefit?"

"Yes, for the benefit of all, not for the gain of a few."

"And what if I say no? How can you harm me?"

"There's a freelance reporter, Mossy Lalor, who's very curious about the Pooka ..."

"Oh, haven't I told you? As of this morning, Mr. Lalor is one of my employees. I'm putting him in charge of publicity."

"Why am I not surprised? You two were made for each other - never let principle stand in the way of profit."

"Easy, Miss Duignan! I'm in no mood to take insults from someone who let her mother die abandoned in a nursing home and who defrauded a charity organisation of close on a thousand pounds to feed her drug habit."

It was Maeve's turn to blanch. "What you have said is the truth," she confessed. "But I've promised Eileen that I'll pay back every penny. And I've already paid back a quarter."

"That may be so," he said, "but it wouldn't look too good if the newspapers got hold of it. We have both a lot to lose, haven't we, Miss Duignan?"

"Maybe," she conceded, "but you see, Mr. Hunt, I don't care. My family is gone, so what does it matter what people think of me? You, on the other hand, *have* to care if you want to become a senator."

"Who told you that?" his abrupt tone showed that her arrow had found its mark. "That Green warrior friend of yours, Michael Vaughan?"

"Does it matter? The point is, Mr. Hunt, this letter only arrived this morning, so whoever ransacked the caravan was out of luck. And here's something else," she took a few black and white photos out of an envelope and handed them to him. "This shows an oak that has already been felled - or rather the branches - with your JCB beside it and this one shows the burnt side of Slieve Brack and this shows the cars and vans that have been dumped by the side of the boreen, cars and vans that belonged to your firm - we have the chassis numbers, so it's no use denying it."

"Who took those photos?"

"Let's say they were taken by concerned residents of this locality."

"Whoever took them was trespassing on my property."

"Property which, as the photos show, you intend to develop. I wonder, Mr. Hunt, how the public will welcome your development?"

"You're not going to pin that dump on me; I never

authorised it," Mr. Hunt seemed genuinely indignant. "Do you know that the county council wanted this bog in front of us for a landfill dump and I turned them down?"

"Why?" she smiled. "Because there's more money in trees?"

"No, Miss Duignan," he snapped, "more employment. A plantation can provide scores of jobs on a long term basis for the school leavers of this area."

"A nature reserve would provide just as many jobs and at less cost to the environment."

"That's more of the airy-fairy economics of your Green friends. What I'm talking about has been tried and tested."

"I can guarantee you, Mr. Hunt, that if you destroy this beautiful countryside, I'll make sure that everybody knows about it."

"Miss Duignan, are you trying to blackmail me in my own caravan?"

"No, Mr. Hunt, I'm trying to ensure that you don't destroy your senatorial prospects for the sake of a few hundred thousand you don't really need. The choice is simple: private profit or public honour."

CHAPTER 26

"Hey, are you fellows going to help me with this damn thing or not?" Johnno growled. He was hammering with a stone the lock that held a new chain. The chain was wrapped around a stake fixed in the bank at the head of a narrow opening in the reeds. The other end of the chain was attached to the prow of a freshly painted boat.

"Ah, leave it," Gallo stuck his hands in his pockets. "We shouldn't take a locked boat."

"What in blazes got into you?" Johnno demanded. "We're only going to borrow it to row out to Gull Island."

"But you said we were going to the wooded island," Freddy protested.

"Did I?" Johnno pretended to be thinking. "Well, I changed my mind. Now, will one of you help me to liberate this tub?"

"But we sank it last time," Aidan pointed out.

"So what?" Johnno shrugged his shoulders.

"It's not fair to the owner," Aidan kept his voice steady.

"It's not fair to the owner," Johnno mimicked. "What would an eejit like you, O'Connor, know about fairness? Do you know who this boat belongs to? A flaming teacher."

"All the same -" Miller began.

"Maybe you National School boys love your teacher," Johnno scoffed, "but in Fennor Vocational we sort them out. Don't we, P.J.?"

"We sure do," P.J. agreed. "Still, I heard that this tub belongs to Ollie and he's not the worst of them."

"No," Johnno agreed, "if you're fool enough to believe in that malarkey about always trying your best."

"What's wrong with that?" Miller asked.

"If you have to ask, there's no use telling you," Johnno hit the lock another blow. When it didn't give, he pulled in the boat and began to hammer the staple that attached the chain to the prow. The stone bit into the wood, breaking off splinters.

"Don't!" Gallo cried. "That's going too far."

"Oh, F off!" Johnno snarled. "I swore I was going to pay those gulls a visit and I mean to keep my word."

"Suppose they attack you again?" Freddy dipped his wellington in the water.

"They won't if the Pooka isn't around," Johnno continued to hit the staple, holding the stone in both hands.

"They will if you go near their nests," Miller warned. "You can see their black heads stuck up watching us already."

"It was a tern that cut his scalp, not a gull," Aidan broke in, "and terns don't nest till June."

"My, aren't you the knowledgeable lad?" Johnno jeered. "Who made you an expert on terns, O'Connor? The Dublin bird?"

"I'm not staying here any longer," Aidan spoke decisively. "If you want to go around smashing things, O'Rourke, I'm not going to be a part of it."

"Good," Johnno balanced the stone in his hand as if he itched to throw it. "Go back to the caravan, you little twerp, and complain to Miss Duignan. The only trouble is she won't be around much longer to listen to your tales."

"Why won't she be around?" Aidan turned back.

"Because Mr. Hunt is chucking her out," Johnno grinned. "He doesn't like busybodies."

"She's not a busybody," Aidan protested. "And as for throwing her out, Mr. Hunt only loaned her the caravan till the end of this month. In fact, she expects him to donate all this land for a nature reserve."

"A nature reserve?" Johnno snorted. "She's a stuck-up cow who thinks she can get anything she asks for."

"That's enough!" Gallo warned. "Maeve is not in the least stuck-up. She's a damn nice person."

"Oh, my!" Johnno exclaimed. "So Miss Duignan has an admirer. Did she let you kiss her?"

"Ah, you're just a loser, O'Rourke," Gallo spoke with cold disdain. "I don't know why I let you talk me into coming with you. Come on, lads. Let's go."

"If you go, I'll see that none of you ever gets work with Big Jim again," Johnno threatened.

"Stuff his work," Gallo cried. "Do you think we can't survive without the few lousy quid he gives us? If Big Jim set Mr. Hunt on Maeve, he's nothing but a bloody informer."

Gallo strode away and, much to Johnno's chagrin, the others began to follow.

"P.J., give me a hand with this," Johnno coaxed. "Look, it's almost out of the wood."

"I'm sorry, Johnno," P.J. looked uncomfortable. "I think what you're doing isn't right."

"Why in hell's name isn't it right?" Johnno snapped. "It's that Duignan one that has turned all your heads with her paintings and her talk about the beauty of the bog. All those city gets like to preach to us about nature and wildlife but that's because they didn't have to grow up in the muck and dirt like you and I had. Remember the craic we used to have before she arrived, P.J., liming the goldfinches, snaring rabbits, pelting the swans? What's wrong with that?"

"I'm sorry, Johnno," P.J. refused to meet the eyes of his mate. "I just don't feel it's right."

"Fine then," Johnno fought to conceal his hurt. "Be off with you. Go on!" He watched him hurrying after the others then he savagely attacked the staple and broke it free.

In about ten minutes Johnno was half way to the island, the water in the bottom of the boat sloshing about the heels of his wellingtons. Ordinarily, he would have been afraid to venture out on his own in such a leaky tub but anger gave him resolve. Before him he could see the heathery slopes of Slieve Brack rising to the cairn-crowned summit, while behind him the alarm cries of gulls and terns mingled with the slapping of water against the prow and the grating of the oars.

As the boat nosed into the reeds amid the clamour of circling gulls, he looked around. Immediately his eye fell on something that chilled his blood: the Pooka's body was floating face down in shallow water.

Controlling his panic, he backrowed, stern first, out of the reeds. Once in deep water, he swung the boat around and headed for the landing place, pulling furiously on the oars. Some innate cunning told him that he should tell no one but Big Jim about what he had seen. If word got out that the Pooka was dead, people might blame those who had imprisoned him or set the fire on Slieve Brack. The least said until he was safely in England the better.

EPILOGUE

In the brilliant August sunshine seven people paused on the cairn's western rim to recover from their climb.

"Look!" Maeve swept her arm in a wide arc that included Eastersnow, the river, Lough Glin, the distant mountains and Lackendarragh. "Have you ever seen anything so beautiful and unspoilt? The men who built this cairn probably saw the exact same landscape we're looking at now."

"If it's so beautiful, why don't you stay on in Jimmy's house?" Gallo asked gruffly.

"I told you, Charlie," she smiled to ease his hurt, "my work here is finished."

"But we've achieved nothing," Gallo pointed out.

"Michael and I are going to Africa in a few weeks time," Maeve ignored the criticism. "It's something I've always wanted to do and now that Mr. Hunt has acceded to our demand -"

"He's what? What did you say? Has he?" a chorus of excited voices made her pause.

"Oh, didn't I tell you?" she pretended to be surprised.

"You know you didn't," Eithne was trying her best to remain calm.

"Go on!" Aidan encouraged. "Don't hold out!"

"Well," Maeve paused dramatically, "Michael drove down specially this morning to give me the news."

"What news?" P.J. demanded impatiently.

"Eastersnow and Slieve Brack are going to be designated by the government as a nature reserve," Maeve allowed a grin to spread across her face.

"Yes! Right on! Cool! Deadly!" they shouted their elation. Freddy and Aidan jumped up and down and Miller threw his arms around Eithne.

138

"Won't Big Jim blow a gasket?" Gallo observed gleefully.

"And Johnno too," Miller added.

"Johnno is on his way to England," P.J. said. "He got a lift up to Dublin this morning with Big Jim. I think they're both taking the ferry."

"Good riddance," Miller cried, punching the air with his two fists. "We won!"

This set the boys into a new outburst of jubilation.

"Wait!" Maeve held up her hand for silence. "There's only one fly in the ointment: Mr. Hunt isn't including Lackendarragh Wood, though he has agreed to sell it for two million, if the government can come up with the money."

"But they'll never do that," Gallo sounded glum.

"You may be damn sure they won't," P.J. concurred.

"Don't get discouraged," Maeve told them. "All of you campaigned for the nature reserve and in spite of the nay sayers and the Doubting Thomases, you pulled it off. Every one of you played an adult's part, carrying placards, writing to the papers, taking photos, ringing politicians and daubing slogans on walls - isn't that right, P.J.?"

There was an outburst of laughter at this.

"But it was you that made the real difference," Eithne observed. "Everybody knows about Easternsnow and the Pooka because of your pictures."

"Daddy showed us the review of your exhibition in the *Sunday Independent*," Aidan broke in. "Your picture of the Pooka looking up at the oak trees was shown above it. That's my favourite one."

"If you keep on like this, you'll give me a swollen head," Maeve laughed. "Anyway, what I wanted to say is this: Mr. Hunt has agreed not to cut down any more oaks for the time being, and I think it may be possible to get E.C. funds to restore the mansion. If so, you could use it as an interpretive centre - you can, of course, use Jimmy Mac Dermott's house in the meantime. So there's your next campaign, persuading the government to shell out two million for Lackendarragh Wood."

"Will Tom Hunt become a senator now?" Miller asked.

"Probably," Maeve said, "if the party he supports wins the next election. But if he holds out for two million, you can use that against them. Call them the 'Fat Cat Party'! Anyway, he's being generous with the nature reserve."

"Down here!" Aidan suddenly called out. "Your picture, Maeve!"

They all hurried to the recess and, sure enough, the water colour of Maeve with the Pooka was resting in its old spot, facing the nest.

"He must still be alive," Aidan exclaimed.

"How could he be?" Freddy objected. "Doesn't everyone know that Big Jim and Johnno did away with him?"

"No, they didn't," P.J. informed him. "Johnno told me that before they searched the caravan back in May they found a blanket in Jimmy Mac Dermott's byre and that's the last trace they had of him."

"Why didn't you tell us this before?" Maeve asked.

"Because Johnno told me not to," P.J. said. "He didn't want you to find out he was near the caravan. Now that he's gone, I reckon it doesn't matter."

"Maeve, do you think the Pooka still sleeps here?" Aidan looked at her with glistening eyes.

"Yes, Aidan, I'm sure he does," she laid her hand on his shoulder, "just as I'm sure that he rides on a stag from Harte's

140

Cullen to Lackendarragh each evening and sings to himself in all the mingled voices of the wilderness. You see, when the people who built this cairn were alive they believed that after death one's spirit could enter the body of a deer or a trout or a grouse - or even a falcon like that one hovering over there. Maybe that falcon is the Pooka keeping an eye on us."

"Or he could be still a boy, just like he was," Aidan carefully picked up the water colour. "Isn't that so?"

"Indeed it is," Maeve agreed. "In this wonderful, crazy world, anything is possible."